D0362358

For the
Strength of You:

Triple Crown Collection

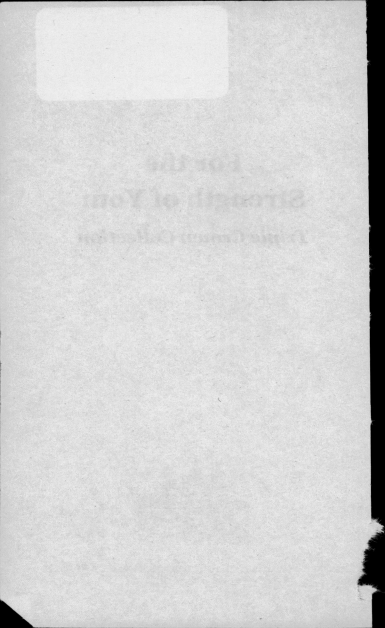

For the Strength of You:

Triple Crown Collection

Victor L. Martin

www.urbanbooks.net

Urban Books, LLC
97 N18th Street
Wyandanch, NY 11798

For the Strength of You: Triple Crown Collection
Copyright © 2005 Triple Crown Publications LLC

This title is published by Urban Books, LLC under a
licensing agreement with Triple Crown Publications
LLC.

All rights reserved. No part of this book may be re-
produced in any form or by any means without prior
consent of the Publisher, except brief quotes used in
reviews.

ISBN 13: 978-1-62286-994-7
ISBN 10: 1-62286-994-X

First Trade Paperback Printing (August 2005)
Printed in the United States of America

10 9 8 7 6 5 4 3 2 1

*This is a work of fiction. Any references or similarities
to actual events, real people, living or dead, or to
real locales are intended to give the novel a sense of
reality. Any similarity in other names, characters,
places, and incidents is entirely coincidental.*

Distributed by Kensington Publishing Corp.
Submit Orders to:
Customer Service
400 Hahn Road
Westminster, MD 21157-4627
Phone: 1-800-733-3000
Fax: 1-800-659-2436

Dedications

I'll let the songs speak for my feelings:

Sandra J. Martin (Mom) = B.I.G.: "Sky's the Limit"

Angie R. Martin (Sis) = Ja Rule and Mary J. Blige: "Rainy Dayz"

Dominique A. Covington (Nephew) = Slick Rick: "Hey Young World"

Janayia A. Martin (Niece) = Keith Murray: "The Most Beautifullest Thing"

Tremika M. Smith (Sis) = Mary J. Blige: "My Life"

Vickie Stringer (A Blessing) = G-Unit: "Smile"

Kontar Joyner (My Nigga) = Main Source: "Looking at the Front Door"

Kim A. Carroll (My Ace) = Seether and Amy Lee: "Broken"

Keama T. Eason (Princess) = Tribe Called Quest: "Relax Yourself"

My Entire Family = Lost Boyz: "Dedication"

T.C.P. = Lost Boyz: "Get Up"

Theme Song for this Novel: B.I.G.: "Unbelievable"

Acknowledgments

I've been blessed again.

I'm thankful to still have my best friend/typist Kim A. Carroll. Where would I be without you?

To all of my readers that supported my first two novels, *A Hood Legend* & *Ménage's Way*, thank you deeply. There's no me without you.

I must put a plug in for *Complex* magazine for doing the first article about me. Thanks for the publicity.

On days I faced writer's block, it was broken down by tuning in to the Butta Team on WNCU 90.7 FM, the official number one street DJs. While I'm on the radio, I gotta send love to Mary Jane at WQOK 97.5 FM. Thank you for your words of encouragement . . . now drop down and get your eagle on, girl!

If anyone in Havelock, N.C. can reach my right hand man, Shaft, tell him to get at me. I owe you plenty!

Karen Hamilton of New Bern, N.C.: Look what you started and the masterpiece can still be yours. Yeah, I'm still on lock, but I refuse to be broken!

Keama Eason . . . I guess I know the meaning of a true friend. Thank you for understanding me.

To everyone that calls Johnston County home: You know I had to pen one for the Dirty-Dirty.

To all my peeps: Sherwood, Decky, Varis, D.C., Patrick Kent, Pig, Tremain, Casual C., Hands, Pee Wee, Markie, Ant Man, Do-Right, T.J. Williams, Vick Tug, Shawn, Fonz, Shan, Mitchell Holmes A.K.A. Big Chubb, Michael Peacock, Von, Fish, Eddie Davis, Jerome, and if I didn't plug you in on this one, forgive me.

And to all my exes and one-night stands . . . picture that! Yeah, I'm out of sight and out of mind . . . for now.

I'll stay humble and I'll stay true. Thank you all for believing in me.

Chapter 1

Selma, North Carolina

REDWOOD VILLAGE APARTMENTS
ATTENTION: NO TRESPASSING
NO LOITERING
NO SOLICITING
ANYONE SEEN IN VIOLATION OF THESE RULES
WILL BE ARRESTED

Friday, July 4th weekend . . .

"Yo, Anshon!" Fe-Fe snorted into the crack of the back door, with snot dripping over her ashy black lips. "It's me, nigga. Fe-Fe. Where you at, yo?"

Anshon was pissed. His dick was hard, and all he wanted to do was fuck Constance, his bad-ass white chick, who lay in the bed waiting for him.

"Anshon, it's me, Fe!" Fe-Fe yelled again, her lips plastered into the crack of the door.

Anshon took his 9 mm off the kitchen table and placed it in the waistband of his sweat pants. He yanked the back door open and Fe-Fe stumbled inside.

"My nigga." Fe-Fe grinned, with slob sliding down the side of her mouth.

Anshon closed the door and Fe-Fe stood up straight. She pulled the belt of her dingy yellow raincoat tight around her tiny waist, reached in her back pocket, and snorted again, "I got some dough, nigga, and I ain't have to suck that much dick and shit. Look." She cupped her hands and showed him a ten-dollar bill and five dollars in change. There were a few bottle caps in the mix, but after she took them out, she handed him the money. "On the real, a bitch needs a twenty spot."

"A twenty spot?" Anshon frowned, reluctantly taking her money. "You ain't suckin' my dick and shit. With all these ma'fuckin' quarters, yo' ass gotta be short."

"Look," Fe-Fe said, looking around the room. "You know I be having to give all my money to my cousin, the one who got my kids and shit. I'm good for it, though, for real. Soon as my check come in next month, I'ma hit you up."

Anshon shook his head. Fe-Fe always had an excuse why her money was short. "Don't come up short no damn more!" he snapped, reaching into the carpenter pocket on the side of his sweat pants and pulling out two vials of crack.

Fe-Fe's whole face lit up. "Boy, you know how it is. I ain't got my check yet." She took the two vials into her hand. "This is that good shit, right? That shit Jinks OD'd off of?"

"Somethin' like that," Anshon said, annoyed and wanting Fe-Fe to leave. Opening the door, he frowned at her. "Bounce 'fore my girl come down here trippin'."

"That is a bad-ass white bitch you got." Fe-Fe wiped the string of snot dripping from her wet nostrils with the back of her hand and snorted what she could back into the bridge of her nose. "She damn near looks like that Brittney Spears trick. But you know I look better than that ho, right? Humph, don't sleep." Fe-Fe snapped her fingers and twirled around. "Ain't no pussy like a black woman's pussy. Word up, you oughta come through and see about a bitch one day." Fe-Fe winked and turned to walk away.

"Be good, Anshon," she yelled over her shoulder, happy that she had what she came for.

It had only been six months since Anshon hit the streets, after doing a two-year stint. His dough was low, and every little bullshit penny counted. Locking the door behind Fe-Fe, he unballed the ten-dollar bill and counted out the change. *Fuckin' chicken*, Anshon thought while throwing the money into his pocket.

"I'm so sick of this bullshit," he moaned as he headed up the stairs to Constance. "But a nigga gotta eat."

Young Buck's "Shawtie Wanna Ride" played from behind the closed bedroom door. Anshon stroked his dick as he thought about Constance being spread eagle, dripping wet and waiting on him. He turned the knob and opened the door.

Constance was standing with her back to him, dressed in a pink Nike T-shirt with nothing underneath, moving her head to the music and ironing her green Department of Corrections uniform.

"What you doin'?" he asked her, lifting the shirt above her waist and pressing his hard dick into her apple bottom ass. One of the things he liked about her was that she had a sista's ass and she never tripped off no black and white shit. Her mouth wasn't on fire like some of the black chicks he fucked here and there. And Constance understood that there was a distinct difference in a nigga being broke and one on the come up. Anshon was sure that a sista would've fronted on him a long time ago.

"You know I gotta go to work," Constance said, pressing the iron into the crease of her pants.

Anshon took two of his fingers and played in her wetness. "Let me hit it real quick."

"Why it gotta be quick?" she smiled, cutting the iron off and yanking the cord from the socket.

"Oh, you want some of this dick?"

"That's what it is?" she teased.

"You tell me what it is." Anshon took his gun from his waist and placed it on the nightstand. Slowly, he started kissing the back of Constance's neck while bending her over. She placed both of her hands on the ironing board and he dropped his pants. He parted her vaginal lips with his dick. Sliding his dick in, he started pounding hard and intense strokes into her wetness.

"You better kill this pussy!" she moaned, as Anshon flicked his fingers across her clit.

"Damn, this is why I started fucking with you."

"Why?" he asked.

"'Cause you know how to work that big dick." She started throwing her ass and working her pussy against his shaft.

"I was in prison when you started fuckin' me, C.O. Connelly," he said sarcastically, "So, what made you think that I had a big dick?" Anshon bit the inside of his cheek in an attempt to fight off the nut he felt creeping up.

"'Cause I watched you in the shower. You ain't never gun me down or beat your meat in front of me. I had to see it somehow," she said.

"So you saw it and what?"

"And this . . ." Constance turned around toward Anshon, causing his dick to slip out. She got down on her knees and started hittin' him off with some head. Sucking her dripping juices off his dick, she took her right hand and started tickling his balls.

Anshon's neck rolled back as his nut broke loose. "God damn you!" he moaned, grabbing a fistful of her auburn hair and pushing his dick further into her mouth. Constance grabbed both of his tight ass cheeks and swallowed his nut.

"You like that shit, don't you?" She smiled, wiping the corners of her mouth and getting off her knees.

"That's wassup," he said, pulling his pants up.

She kissed him on the cheek. "You gonna spend the night?"

"Nah."

"Please." She placed her uniform in the crook of her arm.

"Stop worrying. I'll be here when you get off work. I gotta go check on my sister Tammy. She's been calling me to come through."

"I love you, Anshon," Constance said, hugging him.

"You don't love me." He smirked, squeezing her ass. "You love this dick."

***

After showering and changing into the extra set of clothes he kept at Constance's crib, Anshon jumped in his black and slightly rusted '72 Chevy convertible. He placed his work, which consisted of an eight-ball of crack and a bundle of dope, inside his glove compartment and locked it. Anshon knew it was a dumb move to be riding with vials of crack on him, but he was hoping to run into one of the local hustlers or street runners who were looking to push a li'l weight for the 4th of July weekend.

Slowly, he cruised down Lizzie Street, poppin' his hydraulics and taking in the sights. It was 2:00 a.m., and Selma, North Carolina was live. Firecrackers were blazing the sky, the scent of purple haze floated in the air, and everybody who wasn't outside on their porch was in the local shot house or the barbecue pit—which doubled as a club—gettin' their crunk on.

"Anshon! Yo! Anshon!" A tiny voice yelled from down the block.

When Anshon looked to see who it was, he saw Fe-Fe waving him down. He stopped the car and she ran over to the window. He knew right away that she was high. "Can you run me 'cross town?"

"Run you 'cross town? You runnin' from five-O or something? Don't bring me no ma'fuckin heat, Fe- Fe."

"Come on now." Fe-Fe frowned. "I wouldn't go out like that. On the strength of your sister Tammy, if nothing else."

Knowing that Tammy was his soft spot, Anshon smiled. "Where you goin'?"

"Sumner Street." Fe-Fe smiled.

He sucked his teeth and nodded his head toward the passenger seat. "Get in."

"You ain't hittin' the block?" Fe-Fe asked, closing the door.

"I'm good." Anshon glanced in his rearview mirror before pulling off.

"That stuff you got is the shit. Nigga, I was so high that I thought T.D. Jakes was preachin' to me. Word up, I'm goin' to church on Sunday."

"Yo, Fe, unless you wanna be walkin', you gotta shut the fuck up."

"Oh, I forgot," she said, rolling her window down slightly, "You don't like to discuss this shit in the car. But check it—" She licked her ashy lips. "When you gon' let me give you some ass in exchange for some play? You know I'm a dime piece."

"Fe-Fe."

"Yeah?"

"Shut up."

Fe-Fe rolled her neck. She started to get smart but changed her mind. After all, she was the one catching the ride. "How's my homegirl Tammy doin'?" she asked.

"She's getting better," Anshon said, making a left onto Highway 301. "Last week she got a little feeling back in her legs."

"That's good. Tell 'er I said what's up and that I hope she gets better. You know we graduated Triple S High School the same year."

"Ninety-two?"

"Ninety-one." Fe-Fe smirked. "Yo,"—She laughed, taking her long, slim fingers and covering her mouth—"I was the shit back in the day. Sharp as a fuckin' tack. Couldn't nobody stand me, and it was all good. Tammy used to say, 'Fe, they hate you 'cause they ain't you.' Trust me, Ninety-one was a year I ain't gon' never forget."

Anshon nodded his head as Fe-Fe went on running her mouth.

"Yeah, those were the days. Club Eighty-two, The Dead End in Kenly . . . Shaw's Ball Park. Club Kamikaze in Raleigh." She picked her cheek and popped her lips. "Damn, I forgot that one in Wilson. Yo, I used to get my party on! Fo' sho', fo' sho'."

"Was that before or after you started suckin' that glass dick?" Anshon laughed, turning onto the exit ramp.

Oh, this nigga done lost his fuckin' mind, Fe-Fe thought.

"Let me tell yo' broke hustlin' ass one thang." Fe-Fe whipped her skinny neck around to face him. "You might think you on the come up, but you just one step away from the bus, wit' yo' broke-down, nickel-and-dime ass. You ain't pushin' no Fed weight, nigga. Them misdemeanor hits you sellin' is like sugary shit, so when you start sellin' that real deal, you let me know. Until then, fuck you! All up in my gettin' high business. Don't you worry about when I started gettin' on. When the fuck you gon' reach baller status?"

"Hold up, Fe-Fe. Slow ya roll."

"No, you slow yo' ma'fuckin' roll. If you don't like what I'm sayin' then buck, sucka-ass, cross-eyed nigga! You the one creepin' on the come up, not me. Matter-fact," she said, pointing to the street sign, "this is my stop right here."

Anshon brought his car to a screeching halt and Fe-Fe jumped out, slamming the door behind her.

Anshon sped off, rode around the block, and came back. Fe-Fe was picking her face and smiling at a trick. As Anshon rode closer to where Fe-Fe was, he noticed that the trick was Constance's father, Bob.

Ain't this some shit. Anshon shook his head.

"Yo Fe," he called to her. "Fendisha Lloyd."

Fe-Fe looked around and spotted Anshon. "Nigga, is you crazy callin' me by my government all out in the street and shit?"

"Just come here," Anshon hissed.

Fe-Fe placed her hand on her hip. "Don't you see me and my man holding a conversation right here?" She pointed to Bob's chest. "How yo' bamma ass just gon' run up on me? Would you want somebody to run up on your woman?"

"Fe-Fe," Anshon yelled. "Goddamn! Can a nigga apologize?"

"Oh." She smiled. "One minute, baby," she said to Bob. "Let me go see what his ass want."

The passenger window of Anshon's car was down. Fe-Fe leaned on both elbows through the window. Bob was watching her ass the whole time.

"I'm listening." She rolled her eyes, her breath smelling like cigarette smoke.

"Look, I apologize for the comment I made earlier."

Fe-Fe looked at Anshon, and if it wasn't for how cute he was, she would've kicked his ass. His milk chocolate skin, long, zig-zag parted braids, and his nice six foot tall, prison yard build; not to mention his gold tooth with the diamond in the center, was enough to drive even a sober bitch insane. "Long as you sorry for real and you ain't tryin' to play me out, we cool."

Anshon leaned over and gave her a pound. "I don't blame you for snappin'. But if you ever call me a broke-down hustler again, my size fifteen will check yo' fuckin' chin."

"Size fifteen?" She giggled, "You got my coochie tinglin'! Nigga, if you a size fifteen, I'ma rape you."

"There you go with that bullshit." He couldn't help but laugh. "Peep this, though: While I was locked up or even now, you ever hear anybody talkin' about who shot my sister and why?"

"Naw, all I heard is that somebody had robbed her, shot her up, and snatched her stash. What she tell you?"

"That she was switching banks or some shit and withdrew the money to take to another bank. I don't fuckin' know. But once I find out who hurt her, I swear to God, I'ma split their ma'fuckin' wig."

"Yeah, I feel you . . ." Fe-Fe said, as if Anshon's comment carried her into deep thought. "It fucks me up having to see her in a wheelchair, not walking and shit."

"Yeah, me too." Anshon sighed.

Fe-Fe looked over her shoulder at Bob, who now was pacing back and forth. "Yo, Anshon, my man. My future baby daddy." She grinned.

"Baby daddy?" He frowned. "Don't be speaking that shit into existence. We ain't that fly."

"Look, why don't you hit a sista up real quick. This broke-ass white nigga just got paid. He ready to smash and give up some cash. Let me get some of that work you got."

"Get the cash first." Anshon smirked. "And you got whatever you need."

Fe-Fe walked over to Bob, whispered something in his ear, returned to Anshon with the cash, and they made the exchange of two vials of crack and two bags of dope.

"Well, let me go." Fe-Fe stood up and smiled. "I need to go feed Bob's creamy ass some candy. You're welcome to join us."

Anson didn't respond. Instead, he stared at her, hit the hydraulics on his Chevy, and took off.

"Don't cheat, nigga!" Anshon heard as he rode down Lizzie Street. The twins, Wallo and Teck, were sitting on their front porch, frying fish, grilling chicken, drinking Olde English 800, and playing dominos. Except for Teck's eagle tattoo on his shoulder, there was hardly any telling them apart. Football stars in high school, they had a stocky build, stood at five foot eleven, and were a milk chocolate brown. Rocking gold fronts, on occasion they dressed alike. The twins were always into some kind of hustle.

Anshon beeped the horn as he passed by.

"Yo, Shon!" Teck yelled, standing up and waving his hand for Anshon to come back.

Anshon peeked in his rearview mirror and saw Teck. He did a U-turn in the middle of the street and parked in front of their house.

"What the fuck is y'all doin'?" Anshon laughed, slamming his car door. "You fryin' fish and grillin' at three o'clock in the morning?"

"Don't sleep, nigga," Wallo said, getting up from the dominos table to turn the fish and chicken over. "We sellin' this shit. See that li'l spot on the corner?" He pointed to the small white house with the blue lights decorating the doorway.

"Ms. Johnnie Ray's house?" Anshon smirked, giving Teck some dap.

"Hell yeah," Wallo said. "Don't let Ms. Johnnie Ray fool you, 'cause she always giving out *Watchtowers* and shit. That li'l spot is a fuckin' shot house. Niggas is drinkin' and gambling their ass off. And we got a deal with Ms. Johnnie Ray that when ma'fuckers get hungry, she sends them over here to us."

"That's wassup," Teck added. "And don't be fooled. We got more than fish and chicken. Shit, we got black-eyed peas, candied yams, squash, collard greens, rice, and some smokin'-ass red velvet cake that my baby momma, Kristi, made. And you can have all of this for $4.99, fried corn bread included."

"Sounds like a hustle to me." Anshon grinned.

"Hell yeah!" Wallo gave Anshon a pound. "A nigga ain't never been so legal in his life. But in a minute, we wanna get some of that work. You know what I'm sayin'?"

"Money talks and bullshit walks." Anshon smirked as a line of people started to form in Teck and Wallo's yard. "Y'all li'l niggas don't like to pay. It's bad enough that half of the time I can't tell you apart, but damn if I'ma be chasing you for my ma'fuckin' paper."

"Give us a hour, for real, and we gon' get you the cash. Teck," Wallo yelled, pointing to Anshon, "fix my man some food so he can chill for a minute."

Anshon ate and finished the dominos game with Teck as Wallo served the long line of people. Despite it being the wee hours of the morning, people were outside as if it was the middle of the afternoon. Cars were all doubled park, and Teck's radio was blasting Game and 50 Cent's "In Da Club."

"What . . . you wanna do something, Tom-Tom?" Anshon lifted his wife beater above his waist, revealing the butt of his gun. "I been wanting to blaze yo' ass for a long fuckin' time."

Tom-Tom looked at Teck, Wallo, and Anshon, who by now were all standing side by side with their hands on the butts of their nines. Tom-Tom tapped his foot and rolled his eyes.

Anshon whipped out his gun and pointed it. "Apologize, nigga," he said, walking toward Tom-Tom. Once he got in front of him, Anshon pressed the barrel of the gun into Tom-Tom's forehead. "I wanna shoot you so ma'fuckin bad that I can taste it."

Sweat started bubbling on his nose and above his upper lip. "Do you know how it feels to see my sister broken-hearted and in a wheelchair? Do you know how it feels to see her not being able to take care of her kids? You were supposed to have been her fuckin' man and have her back."

"Look, I-I . . ." Tom-Tom stuttered.

"Look-I-what?" Anshon yelled. "Shut the fuck up. I'm talking!"

"Anshon." Fe-Fe ran over and stood in front of him. Her long, thick, jet black and wavy hair was falling over her shoulders. For once, she didn't look high, and if it wasn't for Anshon knowing that she was a crackhead, he would have thought—at least for a moment—that she was beautiful. "Please don't do it." She grabbed his arm and tried to stare in his eyes. "Please. You got too much to lose. Tom-Tom ain't shit. He ain't worth it."

Anshon didn't budge.

"Teck! Wallo!" Fe-Fe turned to them. "Do something!"

"If the nigga buck," Teck yelled, "pop his ass!"

"Apologize," Anshon said to Tom-Tom, breathing heavy, as if he were in a trance. Tom-Tom held his mouth tight and Anshon clicked the gun.

"I ain't sayin' shit," Tom-Tom protested.

"You's a dumb nigga!" Anshon took the butt of the gun and slapped Tom-Tom diagonally across the face with it. The skin above his right eye popped open like unballing paper. Blood ran down his face like water.

"Say, 'I'm sorry'," Anshon growled. Tom-Tom stiffened and stared Anshon down. "You tryin' to punk me?" Anshon took the butt of the gun and slammed Tom-Tom across the face again, causing Tom-Tom's body to wave like a ripple in a pond.

"I'm sorry," Tom-Tom slurred as he braced his weight against the banister.

"Oh, now you wanna be sorry? I tell you what." Anshon had a crazy look in his eyes. The blood-splattered gun was now pointed at Tom-Tom's face. "The next time you tell a lady to suck yo' dick, I'ma make sure you know how to suck one first!" Before Anshon would let Tom-Tom move, he ran his pockets. Anshon took $200 and three vials of crack. He handed it to Fe-Fe.

"Tell her Merry Christmas!" Anshon snarled at Tom-Tom.

Tom-Tom was shakin' so bad from the stinging pain on the side of his head that he could barely get the words out, "M-M-Merry Chr-Chr-Christmas."

"Now get the fuck outta here!" Anshon shoved and kicked him in the ass as he took off running.

Then Anshon turned to Fe-Fe. "Don't bring yo' ass outside talkin' shit no more."

"Whatever," Fe-Fe mumbled on her way back into her house.

Anshon looked at Teck and Wallo. "Yo, y'all got the money or what? I'm out." Wallo handed Anshon the money in exchange for the rest of his work. Anshon got back in his car, started his hydraulics up, and sped off. It'd been a long night, and Anshon wanted to get some much-needed sleep.

"You know what, nigga?" was the first thing Anshon heard in the morning as he listened to his voice mail. It was Tammy flippin' out. At first he thought he heard wrong, until he started the message over. As he did that, Constance walked in the front door, rolling her eyes and sucking her teeth.

"If I was that white bitch you fuckin' or you needed to re-up," the message continued, "I would've seen your monkey ass yesterday. All I know is that you better come over here today or I'ma handle that ma'fuckin' chest."

Anshon had to laugh. He pressed seven and deleted the message. Constance stood in front of him and huffed.

"What's yo' problem?" Anshon sighed.

"You, that's what."

"What about me?" he said, pulling at the waist of her pants.

"Why the hell are prison inmates telling me how you had a gun to Tom-Tom's head, runnin' his pockets and shit, all over a damn crackhead?"

"I don't know. You tell me. Why would you be hearing that all the way in prison? Especially if you work the graveyard shift. Phones go off at eight and lights go out at nine. By the time you get there, most of them niggas either playing with themselves or 'sleep. And by the time you leave, they still in the same position. So, fuck why. I wanna know who told you that shit."

Constance stood there and looked at Anshon. She backed away from him, causing his hands to fall from her waist. "Don't try and flip the script. You just got out of prison and trouble is the last thing you need. Tom-Tom is crazy. You know he runnin' with the Jamaican Mafia and shit."

"Jamaican Mafia?" Anshon laughed. "Please. Tom-Tom is a punk ass. Period. End of discussion, and for the record, don't ever question me about how I handle myself in the street. Understand?"

"Whatever. And another thing." Constance sucked her teeth. "You got fiends coming to my door all times of the night. My kids be here and shit. You gon' have to chill with all that."

"You know what?" Anshon snapped his fingers. "You must have another dick you suckin' on, 'cause you actin' like a chick with a nigga on the side. Now, if I stop doing business here, then I stop coming, period. You make the choice. I don't know what the hell is wrong with your mouth, but you better catch it, before my fist does. I'm out."

"Anshon! Anshon!" Constance yelled, running to block his path as he prepared to leave. "Okay, okay. Don't leave, baby." She pulled him close to her and started groping his dick. "I'm sorry. I'm flippin'. It's just that I don't want anything to happen to you. Selma is a small town, and I don't want no shit jumpin' off. Okay? You accept my apology?"

He pushed her off of him. "Bitch, please," he hissed. "I don't like your fuckin' attitude."

"Don't call me a bitch!"

"Well, stop acting like one!" Anshon pushed Constance to the side and walked out the door.

"I don't need this bullshit!" Anshon hopped in his car and decided to head over to his sister's crib on the other side of Selma. "I guess I'll get cussed out a second time," he said to himself.

As Anshon pulled up to the gate surrounding Tammy's house, he noticed that the entrance was swung open. Instantly his heart stopped and his head started to hurt. He couldn't figure out why the gate would be open when it was controlled by a numeric code.

The dew from the early morning grass splashed across the toe of his Tims. He placed his hand on the knob and noticed that the door wasn't locked.

"What the fuck! Tammy! Tammy! Where you at?" Anshon's heart started pounding. He pulled the gun from the waist of his pants, leaned against the front door, and peeked into the living room as best he could. From the angle where he was standing, he could see nothing. He slid across the wall so that he could get a full view of the room. Once he got to the archway, he squatted down, took cover, and ran in there. Nothing.

Immediately Tom-Tom popped in his mind. *I knew I shoulda killed that nigga.*

He clicked his gun. Then he reached for the nickel-plated .38 that he kept in the holster around his calf. With a 9 in one hand and a .38 in the other, Anshon was determined that if somebody had hurt his sister or was setting him up for some shit, this morning would be do or die.

From where Anshon was standing, he could see directly into the adjoining dining room, where he spotted Tammy's feet balled up underneath the table. The rest of her body was hidden by the curio. Tears fell from his eyes as he rushed over to where Tammy was.

He bent down and rested his guns next to his thigh, placed her head in his lap, and felt for a pulse. She was alive.

"Tammy," he called softly. "Come on, big sis, you hear me?"

She snatched her hand back. "Got yo' punk ass!" She laughed. "Teach you for not coming over here when I call you."

Anshon was pissed. "You play too damn much." He mushed her on the side of the head. "I should leave yo' ass right there. Where is your wheelchair?"

"I ain't using that shit! Hand me my walker from the corner over there."

Anshon put his guns away. He helped Tammy off the floor and handed her the walker.

"Why would you play like that?" His heart still hadn't returned to its normal beat. "I almost shot this ma'fucker up."

"No you wasn't." She smirked, pushing her walker toward the marble dining room table. "Yo' ass was f'in-a cry. Why they kill my sister? Boo-hoo-hoo."

"Oh, that's funny to you?" Anshon helped Tammy take a step so that she could sit down. "What the fuck?" He rolled his eyes.

"Oh, please. That shit was funny. But what I'm about to tell you is not funny. I got a call from Fe-Fe. She told me that you put a gun to Tom-Tom's head and shit."

"It was behind her ass."

"No, it wasn't." Tammy frowned at him. "You did that shit because he left me. You can't fight my battles, Anshon. I've been hustling a lot longer than you. And you can't mend my broken heart. Fuck that nigga. Why would you even bust a sweat over his ass?"

"Tammy, I swear I can't stand him. I just can't. I just wanna murk his ass. I know he shot you. I know he did."

"Anshon, drop that shit, for real, and listen to what I want to tell you. I'm done with the game."

"What?" Anshon twisted his face.

"I'm done with the hustle. There's nothing left for me to prove. I've got some loot in the bank, my house is paid for, I have my Mercedes truck. I'm done."

"That's only half of what we can get together." Anshon sighed. "I know I've only been home for a minute and so far I've only been nickel and dimin' it, but come on. We can push some fuckin' weight, get Selma on lock, and serve all these niggas."

"I'm tired of that. I been shot up, robbed, can't take care of my kids, and I constantly have to watch my back. The only thing left is for the Feds to run up on me. And from what I can see, ain't none of this shit worth it."

Anshon sat silently. Tammy continued, "Look, what I want is for us to move to Miami. While you were locked up, I bought a little spot down there. We could move there and have a new start."

"Yo, you trippin'." Anshon got up from the table and started to pace. "Big sis, all that you talkin' is beautiful, but I need to make a few more runs and then I'll be straight. I can't keep depending on you to take care of me. Just let me in, Tammy. Tell me the connect. I know you never wanted me that deep in the game, but you gotta put me on. I promise another year and then I'm done."

Tammy shook her head. "Don't let the game be your demise, Anshon. Please don't."

"It won't. Just put me on," he begged.

"I can't do that Anshon."

Anshon walked over to the table and slammed his fist into it. "What the fuck, Tammy! Why not? Don't you see how hard it is for me? You of all people should know that I don't have shit. Nobody said anything to you when you hooked up with Tom-Tom and y'all started lockin' shit down!"

"That was different, I had to take care of you!"

"You ain't take care of me; you took care of you!"

"Anshon!" Tammy yelled. "I should slap the shit out of you!" Tammy couldn't believe what she was hearing.

Anshon didn't know the half of what she went through. All he ever saw was the gully, thugged-out shit; the glitz, the street glamour, and the ghetto richness. So what that he'd been in prison for two years? As far as Anshon was concerned, doing time was all a part of the hustle. Somehow being behind bars made him just that much more thorough, or so he thought. In his mind, it meant that he could rock with the best of 'em, and this is what scared Tammy to death.

"Don't you wanna be more than a street nigga?" Tammy asked him. "What about your football scholarship? Remember, the one you lost because of the streets?"

"I didn't lose that because of the streets." He looked at her like she was crazy. "I lost it because I did a bid for you. Hell, that wasn't my shit. That was yours. I took the weight because you had kids. It was my first offense and it wasn't that much shit. I was supposed to get probation, remember? But instead, I got two years upstate. And what you get?" He looked around the dining room. "You got paid."

"Nigga, do you know what I did for you?" Tammy stood on her feet as best she could. "I took care of yo' black ass when Mommy died. We didn't have shit, not even a pot to piss in and a cracked window to throw it out of, and you got the nerve to talk shit to me? Our damn daddy didn't even give a fuck about us. Shit, I wasn't much older than you, but I did the best I could with what I had. I'm the one who busted my ass off a two-dollar waitress's salary to take care of you. I wasn't your mother; I was your sister!" Tammy broke down and started crying. "Triflin'-ass, ungrateful nigga!"

She had been only eighteen when their mother died. Anshon was twelve. Their father had remarried and wanted nothing to do with them, forcing Tammy to take care of Anshon on her own. She started as a waitress at the Waffle House, and although what she made wasn't much, it was just enough to help her make ends meet. Plus, the customers loved her, and those who knew her situation always gave her good tips.

Tom-Tom was new in town and had just moved to Selma from Raleigh. From his gear alone, everyone could tell he was a drug-dealin' street nigga. Every night Tom-Tom ate dinner at the Waffle House, and he always made sure to sit in Tammy's station. His pockets were laced, so he was sure to always compensate Tammy for her service.

After a while of waiting on him, Tammy started checkin' for him a little bit, but knowing that he sold drugs, she knew she couldn't be bothered with him.

"Wassup, shawtie?" Tom-Tom greeted Tammy as he sat down at the counter.

"May I take your order?" Tammy sucked her teeth.

Tom-Tom smiled. *Oh, she got an attitude.* "If I give you my order, can you handle it?"

"Depends if we got it."

"Well, look. How about you and me tonight at seven? I come by and pick you up and we go out."

"Boy, is you crazy?" She flipped, "Hell naw! I know what's up with you, and I ain't goin' out with no street-runnin' drug nigga."

"Whoooa, slow it the fuck down. You don't know me. I was trying to kick it to you because I thought you were kinda fly, that's it. Don't get it fucked up. You ain't all that. Better take that shit down."

"Well . . ."

"Well nothing. This was a bad idea." Tom-Tom got off the stool he was sitting on and left.

It was a week before he came back. When he walked in the door, he walked in with three of his partners. He looked at Tammy, cut his eyes, and walked the other way.

"Damn, Javette," Tammy said to one of the other waitresses. "He's going to your station. I really want to apologize for the way I tripped the other night. Please let me have that table. I'll give you the tip, whatever it is."

"Shitttt, hell yeah then," Javette agreed. "Them drug niggas be wantin' too much anyway."

Tammy walked over to Tom-Tom's table. "Hello. My name is Tammy. May I take your order?"

"Grits, eggs, and steak," Tom-Tom said, not once looking up at her. "Give everybody else what they want. That is, if you can handle that. Last thing we need is a ho trippin' and shit." He chuckled and glanced at his partners.

"First of all," Tammy snapped, "I ain't a ho, ho. And second of all, I apologize for trippin' on you the other night. I was wrong, and I'm woman enough to admit that."

Tom-Tom laughed. "A'ight, li'l mama. I'ma let it go, 'cause I like how feisty you are. So what about tonight?"

"Tomorrow, at seven."

"Bet, tomorrow."

After that, Tammy and Tom-Tom saw each other every day. She loved him, and without meaning to, he began to love her, which was why it took him a little over a year to ask her to transport for him. At first Tammy told him no, but as time went on, the harder it was to make ends meet. So eventually, Tammy took Tom-Tom up on his offer and began running the drug line from Selma to D.C. and back again. During the next couple of years, they were a team, and their reputation preceded them all along the Eastern seaboard.

During one of her runs to D.C., Tammy came back and Tom-Tom was in jail. He'd been caught with an unregistered firearm, and because this wasn't his first offense, the judge gave him five years hard labor, leaving Tammy to run the show.

She did well for a while. Shit was going off without a hitch, until the night that she and Anshon were stopped alongside of Highway 301.

Anshon had just turned eighteen when he and Tammy were pulled over by the police in Raleigh. The police ran the plates, and Tammy's car came back with over a hundred parking tickets, causing the police to have to seize the car.

Anshon became nervous because he knew what Tammy had tucked beneath the seats. He knew Tammy could never go to prison, because she now had two little mouths to feed.

Anshon's niece and nephew were all he could think about. He couldn't see them suffer without a mother the way he did. So, he grabbed the shit and jumped out the ride with over 200 grams of coke. The police caught him only minutes later.

Tammy hired the best lawyer she could, but the best deal they got Anshon was a two-year bid. Tammy always felt guilty about her brother's situation. To the best of her ability, she repped for her two niggas on lockdown, Tom-Tom and Anshon.

Tammy played the game as best she could, and it was all gravy until she went to the Redwood Village apartments seven months ago to collect her dough and was robbed for $287,000. She had been left in the middle of the parking lot with six bullets burning in her back.

Tammy stood up straight, but she could feel her knees getting weak. For a moment, Anshon forgot about her not wanting to let him deeper into the game. He just couldn't believe that she was standing on her own . . . and for so long.

"Walk," he said, almost in a whisper. "You can do it." As soon as he said that, her knees gave way and she fell to the floor. "Tammy!" Anshon said in a panic, holding his hand out to help her up.

"I don't need your help!" She pushed his hand away. Sitting up, she grabbed the edge of the table and pulled herself up into the chair. Tammy looked at Anshon and tears ran from her eyes. She could see his life flash before her, and if witnessing her crippled life without her children wasn't enough for him, then she needed to give Anshon exactly what he wanted . . . the game.

"I'll set up the first run." Tammy swallowed hard. "Introduce you to the connect, let him make the choice of whether he wants to work with you or not, and then I'm out. Understand?"

"Yes." Anshon was trying not to smile, but he couldn't help it.

"But first, I have to share some things with you about the game."

"What?"

"If you would shut up."

"My fault." He smiled.

Tammy couldn't stand it when Anshon smiled, because his dimples would light up his face, and when that happened, she couldn't stay mad at him long.

"Anshon," she said, reaching for his hand, "listen closely. I want you to know that the higher you are and the more you serving, the worse niggas get. Niggas that you ain't never seen or knew about come for your throat. Two of the most important things I want you to know are: One, you can protect yourself from your enemies, but you need God to shield you from your friends. It's always the ones you least expect. And two, keep your come up on the low. Don't buy a whole buncha new shit. Keep that Chevy and ride that ma'fucker to the ground. Don't trick your money away. Keep the white bitch suckin' ya dick. Don't give no credit, and don't shit where you sleep."

"That's more than two, Tammy."

"Shut up." She laughed. "I'm just telling you. This is how you run the game. Quietly. Trust me, it'll keep you alive."

Chapter 2

Six months later . . .

"Constance!" Teck yelled into the phone, sitting on his front porch, watching Anshon ride by, with the music from Anshon's brand new and minted '77 Chevy leaving an echo behind.

Instantly Teck became pissed. "What the fuck you mean, you don't know where that nigga keeping his stash? He floating around with a mouth fulla ice and platinum and a brand new fuckin' Chevy, plus I hear he just bought a brand new double wide, tucked away in the country somewhere. Now tell me what the fuck is goin' on! I already told my brother not to fuck wit' yo' crazy ass!"

"Don't worry about me and Wallo," she snapped, ready to hang up on him. She was sick of Teck calling and harassing her. "Plus, I already told you that I don't know where his stash is. And furthermore, I'm at work and I don't have time for this bullshit! Not to mention, Anshon don't be staying with me like he used to."

"I tell you what," Teck said, as he noticed Fe-Fe crossing the street. "If you don't find out about the dough, I'ma slit your throat." He hung up.

"Yo, Fe," he called to her from across the street. "Where you goin'?"

She looked at him and rolled her eyes. "I'm goin' to Doughnut's."

"That fat fuck." Teck laughed. Doughnut was a local weed hustler who ate all his money away.

I know this nigga ain't fuckin' Fe-Fe, Teck thought, *Unless he done stepped his game up and selling more than weed.*

"Wallo," Teck yelled to his brother, who was in the house, watching *Sports Center.* "Come on, let's go see what the fuck Doughnut's up to. 'Cause if the nigga got some cash, we gotta make plans to snatch it."

Wallo walked out of the house and onto the porch, dressed in a baggy pair of jeans, a thick gray hoodie, and some Tims. "How did you know I was going over to Doughnut's?"

Teck looked at his brother like he was crazy. "What are you talking about? I'm the one who told you let's go to Doughnut's."

"Oh." Wallo sucked his teeth. "I'm going over to Doughnut's now. This nigga got a trick over there. We 'bout to run a serious fuckin' train." He grabbed his dick. "And I swear I can't wait to fuck this freaky bitch. Word up, I know this shawtie gonna be all the way live!"

Before Teck could comment, Anshon pulled up. Teck bit the inside of his jaw as he noticed Tammy sitting in the front seat.

Damn she looks good, he thought.

"What up, dawg?" Teck said to Anshon.

"You, nigga." Anshon grinned, showing his brand new platinum teeth.

"Oh, a nigga got new fronts." Wallo laughed, pointing to Anshon's mouth, walking toward the car. When he stood next to the passenger side of the car, he leaned in and gave Tammy a kiss on the cheek. Then he said to Anshon, "Yo' I'm on my way to Doughnut's. He got a li'l jump off 'bout to blaze the spot."

"Y'all still into that shit?" Anshon frowned.

"Don't sleep, nigga." Teck shook his head. "You don't run a train every day."

"A train?" Tammy curled her upper lip.

"That ain't nothin' you gotta worry about, li'l mama," Teck said, staring at Tammy. She looked so pretty in her white fox with the matching headband that instantly his dick was hard.

The mid-February cold seemed to fit Tammy quite well. Despite her being crippled, Teck wanted to push up on her.

Tammy could feel Teck's vibe, but instead of her being at ease that this fine-ass, tall chocolate cutie was trying to kick it to her, she cringed. The stare in his dark brown eyes scared the hell outta her. She hadn't felt such an intense feeling of fright since she was gunned down and left for dead.

Closing her eyes, Tammy began to flash back to the day she was shot. She could see herself laying in a pool of her own blood, drowning, as the shooter, on his knees, bent over and whispered in a raspy voice, "I'm sorry." Then he kissed her on her forehead as she lay there almost lifeless.

As he went to turn his back, Tammy mustered up enough strength to pull at the hem of his black T-shirt. He had a ski mask on, and she desperately wanted to pull him to the ground so that she could see his face. But all she could manage to do was rip the collar of his shirt, causing the neck to stretch out of shape, revealing a tattoo of a bald eagle. It was a tattoo that she felt would be etched in her mind forever.

"I'm ready to go, Anshon," Tammy said, shaking herself from her flashback as she opened her eyes.

He looked at her, perplexed. "I thought you wanted to talk to Teck about locking down this block for us."

"Naw, maybe later. My head is starting to hurt."

Feeling uneasy, Teck stepped back from the car. "Holla at me later, Anshon. A'ight?"

"Yeah," Anshon said, slightly embarrassed by his sister's behavior. "I'll holla in about an hour." They pulled off.

"What was that about?" Anshon said as they turned the corner.

"Nothing," Tammy snapped. "It's just time for me to move to Miami."

"Naw, don't give me that bullshit. You had something on your mind. Spill it."

Tammy took a deep breath. "Looking at Teck made me think about when I was shot."

"How?"

"His stare," she said, looking out the window and nervously playing with her hands. "Something about Teck's eyes reminded me of the guy who shot me. Then I started having flashbacks of the eagle tattoo on his shoulder."

"Whose shoulder? Teck?"

"No." Tammy's bottom lip started to shake. "The shooter."

Anshon was confused. "How did you see the shooter's shoulder? I thought you played dead."

"I did, but before I played dead, I yanked the hem of his shirt, revealing his tattoo, but when he turned around and stared at me through the eyes of his ski mask, I swore, Anshon," she said, wiping her falling tears, "that I would never forget that glare he had. The same glare that Teck had a minute ago."

"But, Tammy, how could you see all that and play dead?"

"Because after I saw the tattoo, I dropped my hand, closed my eyes, and let the blood that kept dripping down my throat slide out the corners of my mouth."

Anshon slammed on brakes as he almost hit the car in front of him. He was trying to shake the visual Tammy had just laid on him. The veins in his neck felt like they wanted to explode.

"I swear to God, Tammy!" Anshon yelled, coming to a screeching halt and banging on the steering wheel. "If and when I find that nigga, I'ma murk his ass, execution style, and that's on my word."

Tears rolled down Tammy's face because she knew there was nothing she could say to change the way Anshon felt . . . and something deep inside of her didn't want to.

"But, Tammy," Anshon said, "you shouldn't be scared of Teck. Teck and Wallo is damn near family."

"Family?" Tammy snapped, "When you beatin' this street, servin' these niggas, and goin' hard for that cake, it ain't no ma'fuckin' family."

"Come on, Tammy, my brother's keeper—"

"Yeah, my brother's keeper got his ass shot trying to set up his own block."

"Yo, that's cold, B."

"Yeah, and so is these streets."

Teck was still feeling uneasy about the way Tammy had reacted to him, but he tried to shake it. He twisted his lips and thought about Doughnut and Wallo.

"Let me see if Wallo's ass found out that Fe-Fe is the jump off." Teck laughed to himself.

"Wassup, Teck?" Doughnut said, breathing heavily as he opened the door. Doughnut's house smelled like a bad flavor of ass.

"Goddamn, y'all some nasty niggas," Teck said, holding his nose and watching Wallo come out of Doughnut's bedroom with his legs shaking.

"That bitch is bad," Wallo said, wiping his forehead.

"Where the ho at?" Teck asked, lighting up a purple haze.

"In the bathroom takin' a shower." Wallo grabbed his dick.

"Who is it?" Teck asked, waiting to hear Fe-Fe's name so that he could fall out laughing.

"Does it matter?" Doughnut frowned. "Long as she lay and let us spray, it's all good."

Doughnut sat down on the couch and switched from BET to a porno flick. Wallo dimmed the lights and sat on the couch next to him. He reached over the arm of the couch and handed his brother two condoms.

"Make good use of 'em." No sooner than he said that did Fe-Fe step out of the bathroom, rocking a navy blue negligee with fake Fendi *F*s scribbled all over. The garter belt was clean, but it had two big holes in it.

She looked at Teck and smiled. Her mouth lit up with two gold front teeth. Teck had to do a double take. From the neck up, Fe-Fe was a winner . . . and from the looks of it, if her negligee was in better condition, her body would also be a banger. She walked in front of the TV and placed her leg on the coffee table, revealing her nicely waxed pussy. Teck couldn't believe it.

"Ready for another round, boys?" She winked at Teck. "Wassup with you?"

"You better go 'head," Wallo urged his brother. "Don't let the crackhead look fool you. That's just her style right now, but word up, she got some bomb-ass pussy!"

Teck grabbed Fe-Fe by the arm. "You better not tell nobody but God!"

Teck walked in Doughnut's bedroom with Fe-Fe and frowned up his nose. Doughnut's room smelled like infected ass. Teck opened the window and motioned for Fe-Fe to sit down on the bed.

"What you want, some head?" she asked. "I don't know what them niggas told you, but this pussy right here"—She pointed between her legs—"ain't a free fuck. Don't get it twisted."

"You think I want some pussy from you after you done let them two li'l niggas run up in you? Oh, hell no."

"Then why you got me back here?" She frowned.

"Because I always wanted to ask you something. Why do you get high?"

"What the hell kinda question is that?" Fe-Fe rolled her eyes and placed her hands on her hips. "What the fuck you sell drugs for?"

"Sell drugs? Please, that ain't even my main hustle."

"Then what's your hustle?"

Teck smiled. "I asked you the question first."

"I can't believe I'ma answer this." She smirked. "Back in the day I used to run with Tammy and Tom-Tom. Drugs were everywhere, and I wanted to try 'em. I was already a weed head, but I wanted to see what crack was like and dope too. So I tried 'em."

"And that's it?" Teck frowned. "That's how you became a fiend?"

"Naw." Fe-Fe held her head down. "It started out two or three days a week, and then it grew to every day."

"You got any kids, Fe-Fe?" Teck asked, sitting on the bed next to her.

"I got twin boys." Tears were starting to roll down her cheeks.

"Who's their daddy?"

"Nigga, you gettin' a little fuckin' personal now. I ain't never had no nigga who wanted his dick sucked to ask me about my kids and their daddy."

"I don't want my dick sucked." Teck stroked her hair. "And I ain't just any ol' nigga."

She held her mouth tight. "Their daddy is whatever nigga had the dough to get me my next hit."

"Damn," Teck said, disgusted.

"See, I knew I shouldn't have told you my business."

"Naw, it's cool. I'm good. Where your kids at now?"

"My cousin. She keepin' 'em until I get my act together."

"How long she had 'em?"

"For five years."

"Don't you want your kids back?"

"Ugly as I am?" she snapped. "I don't want my kids seeing me."

"Ugly?" That caught Teck off guard.

"Yeah, nigga, ugly. Nobody ever told me I was beautiful. That shit always hurt me, and when I was high, I realized that I could chase the pain away."

"I wonder if that's why my mom got high," Teck said, more to himself than to Fe-Fe.

"People get high for different reasons," Fe-Fe said with tears filling her eyes. "Some reasons they can talk about, and some reasons they can't. You think I like being a junkie? I just can't help it."

"I would help you," Teck said, rubbing his hand across her cheek.

"Yeah, right." She twisted her lips.

"I would, but you have to want to stop getting high."

"I do."

"Well, I'll take you to the clinic tomorrow."

"Tomorrow?" Fe-Fe frowned, "Slow it down, nigga. I got to get my hit on for at least two more days. Then we can talk about gettin' clean."

Teck looked at Fe-Fe and shook his head.

***

Anshon was decked from head to toe. He stood in front of the full-length mirror inside his walk-in closet and grinned at his reflection. This was the happiest he'd been in a long time. Tammy had hooked him up with the connect. He was gettin' paid and servin' half of Selma and some of Raleigh while doing it.

He remembered quite well that Tammy had instructed him to be quiet on the come up, but some things he just couldn't resist. His minted '77 pearlized blue Chevy with 22-inch chrome Giovannis and a white rag top was one of 'em, along with his custom-designed, bricked-in double wide trailer, tucked away in the country. This was the fuckin' life.

He bent down while looking in the mirror and tied his all white Air Force Ones. He stood up straight and picked a piece of lint from his winter white hoodie. His blue Ecko jeans were perfect. He slipped on his army fatigue jacket and green Vietnam cap. His long braids hung under the cap and rested on his shoulders, and his thick Gucci link platinum chain set it all off. Anshon couldn't help but smile. It was obvious that he was the shit.

Taking one last look at himself, he was ready to go to the pool hall and get his party on. The pool hall was more than just a place to shoot some 8-balls. It doubled as a small club, located right outside of Selma, and played Crunk music and catered to big ballers. So of course, Anshon had to be in the place.

Silently approving his appearance, he reached for his car keys. As he placed them in his pocket, his cell phone rang.

"Yeah," he said, holding the phone to his ear and walking out the door.

"Yo, Shon, what up, dawg?" It was Teck.

"Nothin'. 'Bout to roll through the pool hall. Yo, I'm sorry about earlier, with my sister. The memory of her getting shot still fucks with her."

"It's all good. I can understand," Teck said. "Why don't you come by and pick us up? Or will the twins be cock-blockin'?"

"Nah, where y'all at?" Anshon asked.

"Doughnut's," Teck replied.

"Y'all still fuckin' with his nasty and crazy ass." Anshon laughed, getting into his car and starting the engine. "I hear his baby mama is a straight freak. He started runnin' trains on her, and this bitch is turned the fuck out. My sister told me that she be hanging out in the pool hall, sucking niggas' dicks and shit."

"Get the fuck outta here!" Teck laughed.

"Word." Anshon cracked up. "A'ight, yo, I'm 'bout to come through. Be outside."

Before Anshon pulled out of his yard, he called his sister.

"Hey, big sis, just calling to check on you."

"I'm good." Tammy smiled. "Just typing."

"On what?"

"Why?"

"Just tell me," Anshon pressed.

"Well, since you wanna beg." She giggled. "I'm writing a book."

Anshon fell out laughing.

"See, that's why I ain't wanna tell yo' dumb ass!" Tammy's feelings were hurt. "Y'all some hatin' asses."

"Whooooa, slow down, big sis."

"No, you slow the fuck down." Tammy had a serious attitude. "This ain't a joke to me."

"I'm sorry," Anshon said. "I'm stupid sometimes. You know that. What's your book called?"

"Forget it. Don't try and get on my good side now."

"Look." Anshon sighed. "For real—for real, I'm really sorry. I wanna know the name of it."

"Okay, but you have to promise not to laugh."

"I swear I won't."

"*Hood Legend*. That's the title."

"Oh, word? That's tight as hell. For real. Keep it up, big sis. You know it's all good."

"Thanks, Anshon."

"Love ya, girl." He hung up. Before he pulled off, he slid in Lil Jon's CD and turned the volume all the way up.

Anshon didn't live as far as everybody thought. No one but Tammy knew the exact spot of his crib, and he wanted to keep it that way. It only took him five minutes to get to Doughnut's.

Teck was outside on Doughnut's porch, smoking a cigarette. "Come on!" he yelled as Anshon pulled up. A second later, Wallo and Doughnut stepped out of the house.

Oh, hell no, Anshon thought, *I never said that Doughnut's nasty ass could ride with me. Fuck that. Plus, I know this nigga pockets ain't clean. He always got some shit on him.*

"Teck," Anshon yelled and motioned for him to come around to the driver's window. Teck walked around.

"What the fuck? You said you and Wallo, not Doughnut. I don't want him in my ride. His ass is crazy, and he always got weed and shit on him. And you know ever since the pool hall started poppin', Selma's finest be stoppin' niggas all the time."

"Your point?" Teck frowned.

"My point is that his fat ass ain't riding in here."

"Come on, Shon. It's all good. He been going through some hard times. He and his baby moms broke up. She got another dude that she be flauntin' right in Doughnut's face. He need to hang out with the boys for a li'l while. I'll make sure he's clean."

Anshon stared at Teck and then he gave him a pound to let him know it was all good. "Speak to his ass first." Anshon said, shaking his head in disbelief that he was even in agreement.

Teck walked back onto Doughnut's porch, where Wallo and Doughnut were standing.

"Yo," Teck said, low enough so Anshon couldn't hear him. "This nigga actin' a little retarded. Ignore his ass. Y'all ready to roll?"

"Hell yeah."

They all piled in Anshon's car and took off.

"Yo, turn that shit up, Shon!" Teck said, reaching for the sound system.

"Nigga, is ya crazy?" Anshon laughed. "You don't never touch the radio in a black man's ride." The entire car cracked up.

As Anshon turned into the pool hall's parking lot, Lexie, Doughnut's baby's mother, watched him ride past her with Doughnut, Wallo, and Teck in the car. She loved to torture Doughnut, and being that she was his daughter's mom, that always made him accessible. Doughnut loved

Lexie, but he made the mistake of bringing the freak out of her, causing her to become a gold-diggin' nymphomaniac.

Lexie stepped out of a tinted midnight black Acura 3.5 RL, with red Daisy Duke leather shorts on, a tailor-fitted red leather jacket that fell mid-calf, red leather go-go boots, a red leather corset underneath the jacket, and box braids, braided with red hair that hung down her back. On her arm was Von, a ballin' nigga from Raleigh who claimed to have half of ATL locked down.

Anshon circled the parking lot and ended up parking next to Von's Acura, where Lexie stood with Von, arm in arm, preparing to make an entrance into the club.

Doughnut felt a lump rising in his throat. As he passed by Lexie, he didn't say anything, but he made sure to bump Von as he passed him. Then he turned around, stared Von up and down, and gave him a look that dared him to say something.

The pool hall was packed, and everybody who was somebody from Raleigh, Smithfield, and Selma were in the house. Anshon bought a Colt 45 at the bar as the twins headed for the pool tables. The music was thumpin' with Biggie's "Kick in the Door."

Lexie was parading around on Von's arm, and Doughnut was watching them as they continued to pass by him. He sipped his beer and leaned against the bar.

Anshon sat with his back to the bar, nodded his head to the beat, and was rapping along with the song as Von came up to the bar with Lexie. Anshon glanced at Lexie, and she winked her eye at him as she and Von ordered two bottles of beer. Anshon twisted his lips, but he had to admit that underneath all that red, she had it going on.

Von looked at Anshon. "Word is," he said, sipping on his drink, "that you the man I need to be speaking to."

"Is that so?" Anshon smirked.

"That's what the streets is saying," Von assured him. "Maybe one of these days I can come through and see about you?"

"Maybe," Anshon said, noticing a li'l shawtie walking past him. She was petite, with a smooth caramel complexion and full, soft-looking lips that were coated with clear MAC lip-gloss. Her waist was small, with hips that flared out over her thick thighs.

Instantly, Anshon's dick was hard and he totally tuned Von out. It couldn't be denied that shawtie was boom-bangin'. She had on tight jeans with Baby Phat in block letters, written in pink, going straight across her ass. Not since Anshon was fuckin' with Constance had he seen such a perfect ass. Without thinking, Anshon grabbed his dick.

Destiny Child's "Souljah" started playing, and everybody in the place started moving to the beat. Anshon licked his lips as shawtie started throwing her ass and dancing in the spot where she was standing. Anshon picked up his beer and started walking toward the dance floor, leaving Doughnut standing next to Lexie and Von.

"You know, if I was your man," Anshon said, pressing his dick into shawtie's ass, "I wouldn't let you out of the house looking like this."

She threw her ass deeper into his crotch. Anshon felt like his hard-on was a ticking time bomb.

"Looking like what?" she asked, still pressing her ass into his shaft.

"Like a dime."

"Oh, no you didn't insult me." She turned around toward him, her mouth twisted.

"Goddamn," he said. "Untwist your mouth." Anshon took both of his hands and pushed the microbraids that fell over her shoulders behind her ears, revealing her name-plated, gold-hoop earrings. "Damn, you look good."

"For your information . . ." She smirked, looking him up and down. "I'm not a dime. I'm a twenty spot, so get yo' shit untwisted. And furthermore, you don't know me well enough to be puttin' yo' dick against my ass."

"Not yet. I'm Anshon. Tell me your name, shawtie."

"Well, it ain't shawtie."

Anshon laughed, "Yo, why you trippin'?"

"A'ight. I'ma stop buggin'. My name is Monica."

"How you doin', Monica? Fine, I'm sure."

"Boy, please."

Anshon laughed. "Would you like something to drink?"

"Yeah. I want a Red Bull."

When she said that, it reminded him of Doughnut being left at the bar with Lexie and her new man.

Where did that nigga go? Anshon thought while he ordered Monica's drink.

As soon as Monica took her drink into her hand, gunshots started to pop. Anshon grabbed Monica and took cover. Everybody in the club hit the floor.

"Everybody put they ma'fuckin' hands up!"

When Anshon looked up, he saw three men, dressed in all black with ski masks on and tommy guns in their hands.

Oh, shit, Anshon thought. *These niggas ain't playin'. They really holdin' us up!*

Just then, he heard a hissing sound. When he turned in the direction of the sound, he saw Wallo crouched down in the corner.

"Everybody stand up and shut up!" the men yelled, pointing their guns.

Everyone stood up.

"Run them fuckin' pockets!" one of the other masked men yelled toward Anshon. From the sound of his voice, Anshon knew it was Tom-Tom.

Damn, I shoulda killed this nigga, he thought.

Tom-Tom looked Anshon in the face and leaned forward while running his pockets. "You should've killed me, nigga."

"Don't worry," Anshon said, tight-lipped. "I will."

"What the fuck is going on?" one of the masked men yelled. "Get that nigga cash and be out!"

Tom-Tom grabbed Anshon's cash, which was only eight hundred dollars, and moved on. Everybody in the club had to empty their pockets. The men collected money, jewelry, and even some guns.

As one of them walked by, Anshon got a good look at his shape, and he knew it was Doughnut. *What the fuck?*

He looked toward Wallo. "That's Doughnut," he mouthed.

Wallo didn't answer him; instead, he nodded toward the masked men, who were walking backwards out the door. Doughnut was the last man to walk out.

As Doughnut walked past Lexie, he grabbed her around the neck and pulled her with him. She started screaming. Von stood there paralyzed.

As if things had been moving in slow motion, suddenly all hell broke loose and the people started stampeding out of the club.

Anshon held Monica close, picked her up, and ran with her. When he got outside, he noticed Teck and Wallo running in front of him.

"Doughnut!" Anshon yelled in a panic. "That was that fat motherfucker."

Anshon unlocked and snatched the door open to the car, throwing Monica inside. Teck and Wallo jumped in the back seat. As they went to take off out of the parking lot, they saw Doughnut standing in front of them, holding Lexie by the neck with the gun pointed toward her head, the ski mask no longer covering his face.

"I can't believe that you did this to me," Doughnut cried to Lexie. "As much as I loved you. We got a baby together. What did I do?

Tell me!" Doughnut positioned his finger on the trigger.

"Oh, shit!" Wallo yelled out the window, "Doughnut, don't do it!"

Anshon was trying his best to get away, but everybody was trying to come out of the parking lot at one time, creating massive chaos. Anshon could hear and smell his back tires burning rubber. Then suddenly his car shot forward, causing him to slam on the brakes. Everybody fell forward, and the car behind him almost ran into the back of him.

Looking in the rearview mirror, Anshon could still see Doughnut holding the gun to Lexie's head. He seemed to be in a blind rage. Police sirens were blaring as they surrounded the crowd.

One of them spotted Doughnut and yelled through the bullhorn, "Take cover!"

Doughnut pressed the barrel deeper into the side of Lexie's head. "Say good night." He slowly eased the trigger back. As he did that, shots rang out from everywhere.

Anshon, Monica, and the twins ducked down in the car. It was at least fifteen minutes before they looked back up again, and when they did, Doughnut and Lexie were both dead.

No one said a word on the ride back home; not even Monica, who'd just realized that she was riding home with a stranger.

Chapter 3

After dropping Monica off at home, Anshon stopped by Constance's, but she wouldn't let him in.

"You not gonna let me in?" he asked her in disbelief.

"No, I'm not. How long has it been since I've seen you? And what time is it? Eight o'clock in the morning," she said, answering her own question. "Go back to that bitch you dropped off this morning and fuck her."

"How the fuck do you know who I dropped off?" Anshon reached his hand through the door and collared Constance. "Bitch, are you trying to set me up? You know just a little too much for a bitch who don't never leave from around here."

"Get the fuck off me!" she yelled, pushing his hand down.

"Don't get killed fuckin' wit' the wrong nigga," Anshon said, letting go of her. "Dumb bitch."

She slammed the door in his face, and he hopped back into his ride and took off.

Anshon was pissed. Who the hell did Constance think she was? He started to go back and kick in her door, but he changed his mind and instead made a few phone calls and put a hit on Tom-Tom's life.

Anshon called Tammy at least five or six times, but she didn't answer. In his heart, he felt like something was wrong. He drove down Lizzie Street and pulled up in front of Teck and Wallo's house. He saw Fe-Fe leaving with Teck and a suitcase in her hand.

"Where y'all goin'?" Anshon yelled out the window.

"This nigga done begged me to go to a program. I really ain't the one, but shit, we'll see." Fe-Fe smiled at Anshon. "You know what I'm sayin'."

"It's all good, Fe-Fe." Anshon smiled, giving her a thumbs up. "Just see what happens."

"I'm taking care of that," Teck said, winking at Anshon.

Anshon didn't know what to say. For a minute, he wondered if Teck was doing Fe-Fe.

Anshon redialed Tammy on his cell phone, and still there was no answer. He revved his engine to race over there, and then he thought about the last time Tammy pulled a stunt and scared him half to death. He had to laugh. He picked up the phone and called Monica.

"Wassup, shawtie?"

"You." She yawned.

"Let me come scoop you."

"You just dropped me off." She laughed.

"I know. Grab some gear. You can shower at my spot. I wanna spend some time with you."

"Come on, boy," she said in disbelief.

Anshon was there in less than five minutes. He beeped the horn, and Monica came outside. She was already showered and changed.

"Look at you, cutie." Anshon kissed her on the cheek as she entered his car. Catching a quick peek of her ass, he shook his head. Just then, his phone rang.

"Hello."

"Hey, Anshon." It was Tammy. "I heard about what happened at the club last night. I can't believe that shit."

"Me either." Anshon shook his head, thinking of Doughnut. "I feel sorry for Doughnut and Lexie's little girl."

"Yeah, me too," Tammy said. "That's why I'ma drive to Atlanta. I need to see my kids. Thank God for Aunt Rosa helping me out with them. Anshon . . ."

"What's up, big sis?"

"I'm moving." Tammy took a deep breath. "I need to be with my kids. These months without them have been hell. Aunt Rosa said I could stay with her. Plus, there's a hospital there with one of the best physical therapy clinics in the country. I could take physical therapy to get the strength back into my legs and be able to raise my kids again."

Anshon felt like he wanted to cry. His sister was all he had.

"I told you I was done with the game, Anshon," Tammy continued. "Now it's time for me to get my life back."

"You couldn't tell me this in person?" he asked.

"No, because I didn't want to cry . . . like I am now," she whimpered.

"Big sis, don't cry." Anshon couldn't look at Monica because he thought that he might break out in tears.

Although Monica had only known Anshon for a night, she felt close to him. She took his free hand and placed it in her lap. He squeezed her thigh and smiled. The tears that he wasn't able to catch fell from his eyes.

"When are you leaving?" Anshon asked.

"Right now."

"What!" Anshon screeched.

"I have to, Anshon. Please. I didn't wanna see you because I knew I would never be able to leave you."

Anshon's heart felt like it wanted to break, but he knew that as bad as he needed Tammy, he knew that her kids needed her more. And given the shit that went down with Tom-Tom at the pool hall, Anshon really didn't want Tammy anywhere around.

"I'ma miss you, Tammy."

"I'ma miss you too, Anshon. I need you to send my things. All I can carry are a few pieces."

"You got that. I love you, big sis."

Constance paced back and forth in the living room of her apartment, with her arms crossed and a mean look on her face. When she heard a motorcycle pull up, she went to the door and unlocked it. Wallo came in and didn't pull off his helmet until he closed and locked the door behind him.

"What the fuck? Anshon came here a minute ago and grabbed me by the collar. I think he knows," Constance said in a panic.

"He don't know shit. Where's the cash and shit?"

"All over my damn living room. Don't you see it?"

He looked around and smiled. He moved toward Constance and began to rub her shoulders.

She pushed him away. "Where have you been?"

"Somethin' came up." He gently grabbed her arm and turned her around.

"I'm so mad at you right now!" she snapped. "You be lettin' Teck talk to me any kinda way."

"Don't worry. I've been getting on him about his mouth. I'm sorry, baby." He unfolded her arms and placed them around his neck as he moved his arms around her waist. "I'ma make it up to you."

"I've heard that one before."

"You like your new car, right?"

"Yeah, and I'm worried about folks asking about my new car. I just made sergeant last week." She smiled.

"So?" He kissed her on the neck.

"So, people are wondering how I got a Benz so soon."

"Don't worry about that." He ran his hands through her auburn hair. "I love you, girl."

She kissed him. "I'm ready to leave Selma."

"I know that, baby." He continued to play in her hair. "Soon enough. Soon enough."

No sooner than Fe-Fe stepped foot in the drug rehab program did she turn around and come back out. "I'ma try to do this on my own," she said to Teck as she got back in the car. "Them niggas in there"—She shook her head—"is some real goddamn crackheads. And if that's how I look, I know I gotta kick this shit."

Teck burst out laughing. "Come on, Fe-Fe. Let's go home. I tell you what: If I catch you gettin' high, I'ma kick yo' ass."

"I can do it, Teck," Fe-Fe assured him. "I just need somebody to believe in me."

"Well, I believe in you."

The first thing Teck made Fe-Fe do when they got back to her house was clean up. The house was just plain nasty, and it didn't make any sense.

Once she finished cleaning, he sat her down and said, "I like you a li'l bit. You seem like you could be cool. But I ain't fuckin' you until you have an AIDS test. I don't give a damn how good you look. AIDS don't have a face."

Fe-Fe sucked her teeth but reluctantly agreed. "You gonna go on the block?" she asked, not knowing, exactly what to say to him.

"Why?" He shrugged his shoulders.

"Because if you want to . . . you can sell from here. I can get the word out through the grapevine that you holding . . . and then you won't have to be all out in the open. It's just an idea, but I guess you gotta go see your girl or something."

"The first rule of the street," Teck said, pulling Fe-Fe on the couch next to him, "is you can never get high off your own supply."

"What the hell is that supposed to mean?" she snapped.

"It means"—He leaned over and kissed her on the forehead—"that if you fuck with my shit, we're done. And then I'ma kill you."

"Shut up. Why you talking dumb?" Fe-Fe said. "I already told you that I ain't gonna get high no more."

"A'ight, li'l bit, we'll see . . . and another thing: I don't have a girl."

Fe-Fe's face lit up. She smiled and hugged him tight.

Two weeks passed, and Tom-Tom was still nowhere to be found, Tammy was in Atlanta with her aunt and her kids, Monica and Anshon were kickin' it hard, and Teck and Fe-Fe had locked down the block. Anshon was the connect, Teck cut up and distributed the weight, while Fe-Fe held the dough. Fe-Fe never asked Teck for anything extra. She took her AIDS test as promised, and most of the money that she and Teck made, she took her cut and sent it to the cousin who took care of her twin boys.

Teck and Fe-Fe's sales were coming in like clockwork. Every fiend in Selma seemed to be knocking on Fe-Fe's door, and nobody ever thought anything of it. At most, they thought that Teck was getting high with Fe-Fe, which was why he was there all the time. A few people noticed that Fe-Fe was starting to gain weight and was looking much cleaner, but her being sober was the last thing on anyone's mind.

One evening, around six o'clock, Teck told Fe-Fe he was down to his last and needed to re-up again.

"You need to chill for a minute," she said to him. "Jealous niggas might become suspicious."

Teck looked at Fe-Fe and thought about how good her advice had been up to now. "A'ight." He reached under her bed, pulled out his money box, and started counting the dough they made that day. He was sitting on a crate in her bedroom when he caught Fe-Fe staring at him.

"What you looking at, girl?" He smiled.

"Nothing," she said, leaving to go to the bathroom.

As Fe-Fe walked out of the room, Teck noticed a hole in the side of her jeans. Although he'd been enjoying her company, seeing her clothes with holes in them made him feel sorry for her.

She came back in the bedroom and sat on the mattress Indian style. Teck started staring at her. Her jet black, wavy hair was wildly hanging loose all over her shoulders. She shook it out, and his dick instantly became hard. She smiled, knowing that he wanted to fuck her, but being a man of his word, he wouldn't dare touch her until her AIDS results came back.

She smiled at him, the gleam from her front gold tooth reflecting out of her mouth. "What?"

"I ain't say nothing," he said.

"Well, why you lookin' at me like that?"

"'Cause I'm grown."

"Well, this my crib," she shot back.

"Oh." Teck laughed. "This here ain't our juke joint?"

"Nigga, you crazy!" Fe-Fe fell out laughing.

Teck enjoyed her beauty even more as she smiled. "Come on and take a ride with me," he said.

"Where we goin'?" She frowned.

"Damn, just come on. You'll see."

As they started driving, Fe-Fe asked him again, "Where we going?"

"Goldsboro," he said, turning onto the highway.

"Who you know in Goldsboro? Going to re-up, huh? I see now that you don't know how to juice the game slow. To me it's like sex. Niggas wanna fuck fast and hustle fast, and neither feels good. But if you hustle slow, you get a feel of it . . . just like pussy," Fe-Fe preached.

I betchu I'm waiting this long to fuck this hard-headed nigga and his dick is fuckin' short and skinny, she thought to herself.

"Fe-Fe, I ain't goin' to re-up. We gonna get something to eat and get you some clothes."

"Say what!" Fe-Fe was stunned. She turned in the seat to face him. "Don't be playing no games with me, Teck. Why you trying to make me feel good, knowing damn well you gonna meet a square and ride past me in the street this time next week? Just because I get high—well, used to get high—don't mean I don't have any feelings!"

She felt like she wanted to cry. She folded her arms under her breasts, smacked her lips, and settled back in her seat. "I don't even know why I'm trippin' wit' your young ass. You gonna be like the rest. Fuck you."

Teck glanced over at her as she looked out the tinted window. "If you would think sometimes before you run your mouth, you might make some sense."

She snapped her neck around. "Boy, please. I'm thirty-one years old. You only twenty-two. I know you don't like me, so you can kill this buying me clothes shit. All you want me to give you is some head anyway."

"Let me tell yo' ass one thing!" Teck said, coming to a screeching halt in the middle of the highway. "I don't want you to suck my dick!"

Cars were passing by and blowing their horns. Fe-Fe was scared as hell. "Teck, please pull over to the shoulder. We're in the middle of the highway. Somebody could run into the back of us."

"Fuck all that!" he screamed. "You remind me so much of my mother that every time I look at you, I think of her. I want you to get clean. If I wanted you to suck my dick, then I would've stuck it down your throat the night Wallo and Doughnut were treating you like a ho and running a train on you. I want you to get clean and do what my mother was never able to do!"

"What's that?" Fe-Fe said, crying tears of joy and fright at the same time.

"Stay alive."

Fe-Fe was crying so bad that she couldn't talk. All she could do was hug him. Nobody ever cared this much about her.

Teck eased off the brake and slowly took off down the highway.

When they got to the mall, he handed her a thousand dollars. "Don't lose your damn mind," he warned. "The ten-dollar spot got some cute shit. You ain't been shopping in Rich's and Belts, so don't start now."

Before Fe-Fe could get a hold of herself, she'd planted a kiss on Teck's lips. He tapped her on the ass as she stepped out of the car.

"Buy some Tiger underwear."

Fe-Fe stayed in the mall for two hours. When she came back to the car, Teck was sleeping.

"Wake up, sleepyhead," she said. "Look at what I got."

"Show me when we get home. A nigga's hungry right now."

Fe-Fe grabbed Teck's arm and smiled as they started to pull off.

They stopped off at a local chicken and rib shack for some food.

"So, you gonna be my friend?" Fe-Fe asked as they ate.

"As long as you stay off that stuff."

She held her head down.

"Keep your head up, Fe-Fe." Teck took his hand and lifted up her chin. "It's up to you to stay clean and let the past go. But I'ma do my part and you do yours . . . okay?"

"Yes." She nodded her head.

When they got back to Fe-Fe's house, she couldn't wait to model the clothes for Teck. As she opened the front door, she saw that the mail had come. She took it out of the box, and the first letter she saw was from the county health office. It had to be the results from her AIDS test. She grabbed it and ran into the bathroom, using the excuse of how bad she had to pee, so that Teck wouldn't suspect anything.

Carefully, she tore the test results open. She wondered if she would be punished for her fucked-up life. She took the letter out of the envelope and read it slowly:

Fendisha Lloyd, the results of your HIV/AIDS test are negative. Because of your high risk lifestyle, please remember to be tested regularly.

"Thank you, Jesus!" she shouted at the top of her lungs.

"Fe-Fe!" Teck banged on the bathroom door. "You okay?"

"I just got my AIDS test results." She snatched the door open. "Negative, boo! Negative!"

She jumped in his arms, hugging him for dear life, while shoving the paper in his face. Glancing at the results, he said, "You making my dick hard, baby."

Massaging his hard on, she smiled. "Why don't we see what we can do about that?"

Teck carried her into the bedroom. He laid her on the bed and then stood up. He cut the radio on, and the D.J. was playing H-Town's classic, "Knockin' Da Boots."

"Damn . . . you look good, Fe-Fe." He got down on the bed and climbed between her thighs, biting her nickel-sized nipples through her shirt.

"Mm-hmm," she purred. "Teck, just be my friend. That's all I'll ask of you. Please, don't lie to me or try to play me."

"So, we a team?" he asked, biting her nipples harder.

"Yes," she moaned, nodding her head.

He rolled to the side and unsnapped her bra. Her heavy double Ds practically smothered his face, but he was enjoying every minute of it.

They fucked hard and long and called out each other's names as the sweet smell of sex filled the room. Each time he nutted, she would pull the rubber off and lick him like a kitten. And yes, he made sure she got her nut too.

He fell asleep as he lay behind her in the spoon position. Fe-Fe felt like a queen laying in Teck's arms, but deep in her heart, she felt it wouldn't last.

Chapter 4

The move to Atlanta was good for Tammy. Anshon missed her during the two months she'd been gone, but he and Monica were together every day, so he didn't feel so bad. Tom-Tom was still missing, but word on the street was that he was seen riding through Redwood Village apartments. Anshon knew it was only a matter of time before he would catch up to him.

"Hey, baby," Anshon greeted Monica, who lay across the floor, studying for her college finals.

"Hey, sugar sweets," Monica said, rolling on her back. "You just gettin' here?"

"Yeah. I missed you." He pushed her schoolbooks to the side and lay on top of her.

"Mmm . . . I know your girl gets the best," Monica hissed.

"Don't play me, mami," Anshon said in his best Latin accent. "You know what I give you is better than what my girl gets."

Monica mushed Anshon on the side of his head. "Don't play with me!"

Anshon laughed as he started feeling between her legs.

Over at Fe-Fe's, Teck was sweeping the kitchen floor as Fe-Fe stood at the stove frying some chicken.

"What time tomorrow will the new furniture be here?" she said over her shoulder. Not only was she excited about the new digs for her crib, but she was even more excited about her new life. It wasn't every day that a crackhead was given a second chance. As far as Fe-Fe was concerned, Teck was that nigga.

"The furtniture'll be here in the morning, baby," Teck said, dumping the dust pan into the garbage. "At least by ten."

The sound of Teck calling her "baby" was the sweetest sound Fe-Fe had heard in a long time.

Leaning up against the counter, Teck pulled out a wad of cash he made that day and started counting it. Afterward, he handed it to her and said, "Put that away. Send half of it to your cousin for your sons, and the other half, I want you to open up a bank account."

Fe-Fe couldn't believe her ears. She finished cooking the chicken and fixed Teck a plate of food. After they had dinner, she led him by the hand into her candlelit bedroom.

"Teck," she said, kissing his pecs slowly, laying with him on the bed and sucking on his nipples, "I swear you the best man I've ever had. I never had nobody to care about me."

He rolled on top of her. "Don't worry about that no more. Just know that I care about you. Now enough of the sentimental shit. I wanna hear this headboard bang against the wall!"

Fe-Fe fell out laughing, and before Teck knew it, she'd rolled him over and slid between his legs, took his dick into her mouth, and was slowly gettin' her eagle on. He let his head roll back and in between seeing stars, he could swear that her tongue felt better than a hot and wet prison washrag coated with melted Vaseline.

"Yo, Shon, what up?" Teck called Anshon on his cell phone, trying to set up a time to re-up. "You got a li'l freak in the secret Bat Cave or what?"

"Naw, I don't fuck with freaks. But since you tryin' to find out what my dick's been up to, I been chillin' with that li'l shawtie, Monica, from the club. Wassup wit' you?" Anshon asked.

"Doin' my ting-ting. Dawg, tryin' to re-up, na'mean?"

"I feel you, but yo, Teck . . ." Anshon hesitated. "I ain't tryin' to be in your business, but you know you can't get high off your own supply."

"What the hell you talkin' about?"

"This shit you got goin' on with Fe-Fe. Yo, you ain't on that shit, is you?"

"Maaaaannn, hell naw. Fe-Fe is clean, dawg. Have you seen her lately? She lookin' good as hell, her gold tooth shinin'. Don't sleep on Fe. Fuck what dem niggas in the street sayin'."

"A'ight, I'll call you later. We can meet up about five or six this evening."

Tom-Tom sat in his beat-up and rusted trailer in Buck Adams trailer park, laid out on his couch smoking a Newport, playing with his dick and watching TV. Nothing was going right. He had no money, his food was getting low, and Anshon had a price on his head.

He put his dick back in his pants, sat up, and started snorting a line of coke. Slowly but surely, Tom-Tom was falling off. He either had to come out of hiding or die.

He couldn't believe what was happening to him. How did the little boy that he helped raise become the one to have a price on his head? After all, Tom-Tom was the one who taught Tammy the game, and she passed it on to Anshon.

"I made you, ma'fucker!" Tom-Tom yelled out as his high started to take effect.

"I'm the fuckin' star!" Tom started thinking about Tammy. "Cripple bitch!" He took his index finger, held his right nostril closed, and snorted a line of coke with the open one. Thoughts of Tammy raced through his mind.

After Tom-Tom left Tammy, she had called him and cried for a month, begging him to come back. But he couldn't. How could he when she had risen to the top of the game and refused to move over?

"Together?" he said to her the day he got out of prison. "Bitch, is you crazy?"

"But how can I give all this up?" she cried. "I've worked too hard. Look, baby, I got two female drivers to run the D.C. line, and all you basically have to do is chill and watch the dough roll in."

"Naw, you think I'ma let a bitch lead me around in the game? You done lost your mind? I'm the one that put you on. Know what? Fuck it and fuck you!" It was not that he didn't love

Tammy, but his heart couldn't take the way she ran the game without him. A quiet, red-head, freckle-faced, two-dollar waitress was slangin' dem thangs better than he could've ever imagined, and to make matters worse, everybody that she was sellin' to wanted to keep it that way.

That's when Tom-Tom hooked up with Teck and Wallo. He'd heard through the streets that they were stick-up kids, the Dirty-Dirty's version of the old DMX, robbin' niggas and bragging about it. He hooked up with them and came up with a plan: snatch Tammy's cash and force her to start over. Then he would regain the hustle and the bitch, Tammy, would fall back into her place.

But he never imagined that the robbery would go bust and Tammy would be shot in Redwood Village parking lot. So, the combination of Tom-Tom, Teck, and Wallo stayed on the low, until the night in the pool hall. That was supposed to be their coming out party. They just never expected that Doughnut was such a crazy motherfucker.

"I swear to God, I'ma kill that bitch!" Tom-Tom said, laying his head back and watching the ceiling. "I'ma kill her!"

Chapter 5

An hour later, Tom-Tom was coming down from his high. He looked out the window and then it clicked. He knew just what to do to teach Tammy a lesson.

He walked outside to the shed in his backyard and took out three bottles of lighter fluid along with a box of matches. "I'ma teach this bitch not to ever fuck with me!"

He jumped in his car and drove over to Tammy's house. Once he got there, he remembered that the gate was controlled by a numeric code, but Tom-Tom was sure that Tammy hadn't changed, so he punched in their daughter's birthdate. The gate popped open.

He drove up close to the house and pulled his car around back. He took the lighter fluid and started to splash it around the foundation of the house.

"This bitch thinks that she runnin' shit! I'll fix her. Sleep well, ya mute-legged bitch!" Tom-Tom sneered, convinced that Tammy was in the house. "Sleep all night and burn in hell."

By the time Tom-Tom was done, he'd emptied three bottles of lighter fluid. Then he stood back, pulled a Newport from behind his ear, and lit it. He took a drag and flicked it onto the grass. The fire blazed instantly, giving Tom-Tom little time to take off.

Anshon and Monica lay across the floor after two hours of hard fuckin' when his cell phone rang.

"I hope your bitch-ass sister's dope-dealin' house burns to the ground, and I hope she sleeps well in it!" a sinister voice said.

Anshon repeated those threatening words in his head. The number appeared on his caller ID as UNKNOWN, and he kept trying to put it all together.

"Oh, shit! Monica!" Anshon said. "My sister's house! I gotta go check on her house."

Monica was in a panic watching Anshon throw his clothes on. "What's wrong, baby?"

"Nothing," he said, zipping his jeans. "I gotta go check on my sister's house."

Anshon jumped in his car and called Teck. He didn't get an answer. Then he called Wallo.

"What up, Anshon?" Wallo yawned. He'd been out runnin' trains all night.

"Nigga, get dressed and meet me outside. I think that fuckin' Tom-Tom has done something to my sister's house."

Wallo rolled his eyes in his head. He prayed that Tom-Tom wasn't turning out to be like Doughnut's crazy ass. "A'ight." Wallo took a deep breath. "Come through."

Anshon picked up Wallo and headed up to Tammy's. When he got there, all he could see were blazes of fire and smoke. The firemen wouldn't let anyone get close.

"Goddamn!" Anshon threw a punch in the air. "My sister could've been in that bitch!" He turned to Wallo. "I know it was that bitch-ass faggot, Tom-Tom!"

"Let's go kick his ass!" Wallo said, pissed off that Tom-Tom would do some dumb shit like this. "Let's go get Teck first."

"Where he at?" Anshon asked, jumping back in his car.

"Where else? Fe-Fe's."

Anshon and Wallo practically flew to Fe-Fe's. They told Teck the story, and he rolled out with them.

As the screen door was still swinging against the frame from Teck leaving, Fe-Fe's heart started to race as she thought about what they might do to Tom-Tom. She prayed that they all came back home alive.

***

Tom-Tom was in his kitchen, paranoid from the coke he had snorted. He kept looking out the window and thinking that the police were coming to arrest him.

"This is some fuckin' bullshit!" he muttered to himself, heading back into the living room. He stopped in his tracks, heading back to peek out the kitchen window. He hoped that Tammy's death would make the news.

"See you in hell, bitch!" He laughed, walking back into the living room. He flopped down on his sofa and kicked his feet up on the armrest and closed his eyes.

He was dozing off when he heard a car pull up outside. His heart skipped a beat as Anshon, Teck, and Wallo shot up his door. He jumped from the couch and took cover.

"What the fuck!"

Wallo walked over to Tom-Tom and threw him on the sofa. "Stupid ass!"

Tom-Tom tussled with Wallo.

"Yo," Tom-Tom stuttered. "I—I didn't do nothin'."

Anshon and Teck broke them apart. Tom-Tom wasn't a small dude, and one on one he would have fucked Wallo up. But Tom-Tom knew he was about to get jumped if he overtook Wallo, so instead Tom-Tom tried to make a break for his .38.

Teck punched him in the jaw as Anshon came from behind and put a chokehold on him.

"Calm down, nigga!" Anshon hissed in his ear.

Tom-Tom continued to struggle with Anshon as Teck and Wallo started raining blows to his face. Anshon wrapped his leg around one of Tom-Tom's and tripped him up. When he was on the floor gasping for air, Anshon pointed the 9 mm to his head.

Tom-Tom rolled to his back as Wallo kicked him in the ribs. Blood ran freely from Tom-Tom's busted lip. As Teck went to pick up Tom-Tom and throw him across the room, he peeked four bottles of lighter fluid and matches.

"Bingo!" Teck said, pointing to the evidence.

"Man, I ain't—" Tom-Tom tried to speak but was cut off by Wallo's left foot to the side of his head.

"Shut up, fuckin' snitch-ass lame!" Wallo yelled.

"Strip!" Anshon said, kicking Tom-Tom in the leg. "Get naked, punk!"

"Fuck you!" Tom-Tom shot back. "You ain't no killer!"

Anshon smiled then nodded at Teck, who started to put some duct tape around Tom-Tom's wrists and ankles.

Tom-Tom started to struggle but ceased when Wallo pulled out a box cutter and put the blade to his throat. Once his ankles were tightly taped and the same for his hands behind his back, Wallo then used the box cutter to cut his clothes off.

"Don't cut the lame!" Teck said as Wallo nicked Tom-Tom for the third time.

Tom-Tom was scared now. He was butt-ass naked and couldn't do shit.

"Hold the fuck still!" Anshon said to Tom-Tom as Teck pulled out a Magic Marker and wrote *DEAD NIGGA* on Tom-Tom's forehead.

He started to cry and mumble. Wallo planted a boot in his stomach then kicked him in the head.

"Now you gonna know what Cain felt like. Pick his bitch ass up!"

Tom-Tom pleaded with Anshon. "Yo, man, chill. I'll leave town. I'll do whatever, man. . . . Yo, Anshon!" he shouted.

Anshon ignored him.

"Man, please!" Tom-Tom shouted, falling to his knees. Snot ran from his nose as he started to crumble. "Please, man. I didn't mean to do it." He sobbed.

"Look, I raised you, Anshon. I taught Tammy the game. She stole my shit. Teck, Wallo, tell 'im. Tell 'im."

"Shut the fuck up!" Wallo shouted.

Teck answered by kicking him in the mouth.

"I got something for your ass!" Anshon said, running back to his car. He remembered that Monica had left her overnight bag in his car.

He went in the bag and pulled out a big electric curling iron. When Anshon returned back to the house, Tom-Tom snickered. He thought Anshon was going to come back with a gun and kill him, but he never expected a curling iron.

Anshon walked in and picked up the lighter fluid, then he walked over to Tom-Tom, who Wallo now had in a chokehold. He took the lighter fluid, poured the whole bottle on top of the curler, and shoved it up Tom-Tom's ass.

Tom-Tom started to scream as Anshon started pushing the curler further into his asshole. Teck grabbed an extension cord from the floor, swung it in front of Tom-Tom's face like a pocketwatch, and threw it to Wallo, who plugged the iron into the socket. Tom-Tom shitted on himself.

The curling iron was making snap, crackle, and pop noises up Tom-Tom's ass. He dropped his head, slob sliding out the side of his mouth, and he fainted—never to wake up again.

"Die slow, ma'fucker!" Anshon said as he, Teck, and Wallo headed out the door. "And that's on the strength of my sister!"

"Boy, what happened to you?" Fe-Fe said, looking at Teck's ripped and blood-splattered jacket. Too afraid to know what had really happened, she retracted her question. "Ain't no need in tellin' me."

"No matter what happens," Teck said to Fe-Fe, flopping down on the bed next to her, "always know that I really care for you."

"Boy," Fe-Fe said, feeling the lump rising in her throat, "be quiet."

"Hey, Fe," Teck said after a few minutes of silence. "I got something for you." He went in the bedroom and came back out. "Here." He handed her a diamond bracelet.

"Oh my Lord! Teck," Fe-Fe squealed. "Jesus!" She started hugging him tight. "What happened to the box, baby?"

"I . . . I don't know," Teck stuttered. "Just accept the gift, Fe. Damn."

"I'll take this gift if you can take mine."

"What?" Teck smiled, watching Fe-Fe unbuckle his pants.

"This," she said as she started giving him head.

"Damn," Teck mumbled. "I should've given you this bracelet a long time ago."

Chapter 6

Anshon was glad the sun was out. He was at a stoplight on New Bern Avenue when he dropped the top with Slick Rick's "Hey Young World" massaging the four 12s in the trunk. He called Monica, hoping that she was up. She picked up on the second ring.

"What up, shawtie? Let me come scoop you."

"Anshon, you heard what happened to Tom-Tom?" she asked.

From Monica's tone, he didn't know if she was asking him or telling him. "Is that a question?" he asked.

"Yeah."

"Oh. Naw," he said. "I ain't heard nothin'."

"He was electrocuted. His insides were out-side of his body by the time the police found him. You know anything about that?"

"Come on now, shawtie. What I look like? I can't say that I feel bad about the nigga being dead . . . I mean, my sister may feel some kinda way, but hell, we all gotta die sometime."

"Whatever, Anshon."

"Yo, I'm tryin' to see you. Wassup?"

She sucked her teeth and blushed at the same time. "Come on, boy."

Anshon smiled. "Fe-Fe and Teck are having a small card party later on, so I hope you know how to put your Spades game down."

"My book!" Fe-Fe yelled at Teck, grinning.

Teck did a double take. "Baby," he said, not wanting to embarrass her in front of Monica and Anshon. "Where's your other cap at?" He pointed to her mouth.

"I wanted to surprise you. I got implants, one porcelain and one gold."

"Let me see," Monica said to Fe-Fe. "You look good, girl!"

"Thank you," Fe-Fe said, covering her mouth. As she did that, her present from Teck slid down her arm.

"Wow, Fe-Fe!" Monica screamed. Anshon and Teck looked at her like she was crazy. "That bracelet is beautiful! Let me see."

"Teck gave it to me." Fe-Fe held her arm out.

Monica looked at the bracelet and her eyes lit up. "This is mine! Where did you get this from, Teck?"

"This ain't yours," Fe-Fe said, snatching her arm back. "My man gave me this."

"That is mine!" Monica said. "My name is engraved on the lock. Look at it closely. That's my bracelet that I was jacked for that night in the club."

Fe-Fe took off the bracelet and looked at the lobster claw lock, and it read *Monica*. Fe-Fe felt like a fool. She looked at Teck.

"I thought this was the jeweler's inscription. I'm sorry, Monica. I thought maybe I had a name brand piece."

"I can't believe this shit," Teck said, looking at Anshon, who had his face twisted. "I bought that shit from the pawn shop. I would've never known that it was stolen." He took the bracelet out of Fe-Fe's hands and gave it to Monica. "Here you go, baby girl. My fault." He turned to Fe. "I'll get you another one."

Fe-Fe sat back down in her chair, embarrassed. This was one time that she wished she was still getting high.

"Girl, you hear what happened to Tom-Tom?" Monica said, trying to break the uncomfortable silence.

"Naw, what?" Fe-Fe mumbled, peeking at the bracelet that was now on Monica's wrist.

"My homegirl, Gina," Monica said, "called me this morning and told me that Tom-Tom's next door neighbor found him electrocuted. The insides of his ass were on his living room floor."

"What!" Fe-Fe screeched, looking at Teck. "Who done it?"

"I don't know." Teck frowned. "What the fuck is you, the law? Don't be looking at me."

Fe-Fe looked at Anshon. He simply turned his head. Fe-Fe sucked her teeth, grabbed the deck of cards, and reshuffled them.

"Anshon?" Monica said. "You seen my electric curling iron? I left it in your car."

Anshon spit his beer out. Teck looked at him and handed him a napkin. "What the hell kinda question is that?" he asked. "I don't keep up with no damn curlers."

"It ain't that deep, Anshon. I just asked."

"Well, naw," he snapped. "I ain't seen it."

The card game was downhill from there. They finished the hand they were playing and then Anshon started yawning.

"I'm getting a little tired. We'll get up with y'all tomorrow," he said, looking at Monica.

Monica lifted her arms in the air and stretched. "Okay, baby."

"Well, I'm glad y'all came by," Fe-Fe said.

They all stood up from the table and walked toward the front door. Anshon and Teck walked outside to Anshon's car, while the girls lagged behind.

"Fe-Fe," Monica said, grabbing her hand. "I got something for you." She handed her the bracelet.

"What you doing, Monica?" Fe-Fe was surprised and tried pushing the bracelet back into Monica's hands. "This yours."

"You can have it." Monica smiled. "The diamonds ain't real, and the gold is just ten karat. I don't need it. You take it."

Fe-Fe didn't know what to say. She kissed Monica on the cheek. "Nobody never gave me nothing. Anything I ever had came 'cause I sucked dick real good or I stole it. So thank you. I really appreciate it, but it's yours, and I don't want it. Please take it back."

Monica could tell that she was making Fe-Fe feel uncomfortable. "Okay, Fe-Fe, but the next time, I want you to take what I give you."

"I will."

Monica kissed Fe-Fe on the cheek, and she and Anshon left.

The next morning, Teck and Fe-Fe were bagging up coke when Fe-Fe asked, "You think Anshon killed Tom-Tom?"

Teck picked up two grams off the table and rolled them in the palm of his hand, making sure they were the same size. He placed them back on the table then carefully picked up a razor. Fe-Fe repeated her question.

"Yo, check this," Teck snapped. "You see I'm tryin' to handle this." He pointed to the coke. "Just mind your business and handle this trap right here. This li'l spot is all we got to worry 'bout. I got a wrist fulla rubber bands, which equals mo' money and mo' problems, and that's more than enough to have on your mind. Don't worry about what happened to Tom-Tom."

"I understand." Fe-Fe smirked. "I understand quite well. Anshon ain't kill him. Both y'all did!"

Teck ignored her and continued bagging up his work.

An hour later, Teck finished and said to Fe-Fe, who was serving a fiend and listening to *All My Children*, "I gotta roll real quick. I need to go and check my brother."

Fe-Fe nodded her head as Teck left out the back door.

It was ten o'clock in the morning. Anshon had just dropped Monica off for her morning classes at the community college. He started to run home, but then he decided to go by Fe-Fe's and check Teck.

"Yo, Fe," Anshon called, rattling the screen on the front door.

Fe-Fe didn't hear Anshon announce himself, but she heard the door rattle. She ran to the front door hoping it was Teck. She'd been unable to sleep ever since she found a bloody ski mask tucked under her bed, along with five different IDs from people that she knew lived on the other side of Selma.

I hope this nigga ain't runnin' no credit card scheme, she thought on her way to the door. *Shit, if white folks locked Martha Stewart up, niggas can forget about it. It's pretty much a wrap, 'cause in a moment, lynching gon' be legal, so I know Teck got better sense than to be messing with white collar crime shit. He better stick to the nickel-and-dime state charges.*

"Teck," she yelled, snatching the front door open. "What is this shit I found?" She held the ski mask out. When she saw Anshon was at the door, she quickly snatched it back. "Anshon," she said, breathing heavy, "I thought you were Teck."

Anshon was so taken aback by Fe-Fe that he never noticed the mask. She was dressed in a tight white turtleneck that hugged her heavy breasts. Her nipples were hard, slightly poked out through her bra, causing the imprint to come through her shirt. She also had on a tight pair of Never Broke jeans that Teck had bought her.

Anshon wanted to grab his dick. It was so hard that it was starting to ache. For the first time, Anshon knew that as long as she was sober, he could imagine fucking her.

Fe-Fe turned her back to him. "Close the door behind you."

Immediately, his eyes went to her ass. He had no choice but to grab his dick. Her ass resembled a brand-new, pumped-up basketball.

Fe-Fe sat down on the couch and Anshon went to sit next to her.

"Where's Teck?" Anshon asked, trying to cover up his hard-on as he sat.

"Good question." Fe-Fe reached over Anshon and grabbed the cordless phone, her 36-Ds brushing back and forth across his dick.

She dialed Teck's number and got no answer. "Fuck this. I was gonna cook, but ain't no tellin' when his ass gonna get here. Can you take me to McDonald's right quick?"

"Yeah," Anshon said, standing up. He placed his hands in his pockets, hoping to somehow hide his hard-on again. "I can go for a few bacon, egg, and cheese biscuits . . . and some fries."

Fe-Fe went upstairs to get her purse and left a note for Teck that she went to McDonald's with Anshon.

"It's cold as hell out here," Fe-Fe said as she got into the Chevy. "I'll be glad when it's summertime."

"Me too," Anshon replied. "I wonder if Teck and Wallo gon' be selling them dinners again."

"Your guess is as good as mine," Fe-Fe said, looking out the window.

Anshon took I-95 then rode it until he reached the rest stop. This McDonald's was closer than the one in the center of town.

They went through the McDonald's drive-thru and twenty minutes later, they had the food and were back at Fe-Fe's house. Teck still hadn't returned.

"How old are you?" Fe-Fe asked Anshon as they sat in the living room eating their food.

"Twenty-two. Why?"

"Just askin'," she said, balling up the wrapper from her sausage biscuit. "Hey, I got another question to ask." She took a sip of her Diet Coke.

"Yeah?"

"Let's say . . . if you was to like . . . um . . . to meet me out of town and didn't know me, would you step to me?"

Anshon had a mouth full of food and quickly picked up his cup of Sprite to wash it down. "I'ma act like I didn't hear that, Fe-Fe."

She rolled her eyes. "Fool, I ain't tryin' to do nothin' wit' you. I just wanna know if you would find me good to look at . . . that's all."

"Oh . . . well . . . if I had never met you and didn't knew your past . . . then hell yeah. I'd step to you with a quickness. Why you ask?"

"'Cause your dick was hard when I reached over you for the phone earlier." Fe-Fe smiled, pushing her wavy hair behind her ears.

"You trippin', Fe-Fe," he said, removing the wrapper from his third biscuit. He peeked at her from outta the corner of his eye. He hated that she knew his dick was hard, but hell, ever since she'd been clean, she was something to look at. Five foot three, 36-26-38, 140 lbs. She was turning a lot of heads, and most, like Anshon, were ashamed to admit it. Fe-Fe was a coal-covered diamond that just needed to be polished, and Teck happened to be the only one to see that she was a rare jewel. Niggas that had tricked Fe-Fe knew how good the pussy was, and a few were now hating Teck because he had Fe-Fe on lock.

He glanced over at Fe-Fe to see if she was still looking at him.

"Let me stop." She laughed.

"A'ight." Anshon stood to leave. "Tell Teck to call me."

As he went to step out the door, Fe-Fe called out his name. "Anshon, thanks for not puttin' dirt on my name. I know you could have told Teck about me tryin' to give you some ass that night when I was trickin' with Bobby at Masters Inn. I know it was before me and him hooked up, but you know how it would look." She hunched her shoulders. "Teck would start thinkin' we up to somethin'."

"That's the past, Fe-Fe, and you still cool wit' me. Just have Teck call me when he get in."

"Okay." Fe-Fe blushed, closing the door behind him.

A week had passed, and still no Teck. Fe-Fe was starting to give up on their relationship.

She was cleaning her living room when she found a shitload of jewelry and more stolen IDs under her couch. *What the fuck is going on here?* she thought to herself.

She was holding the jewelry in her hand when Teck walked in. She quickly threw it back under the couch. When she looked up, Teck was standing over her.

"What you lookin' for?" he asked.

"Nothin'," she snapped. "Where the fuck you been?"

"Out!"

"Well, since you been out, you can stay the fuck out! Nigga, I'm sick of y'all big-dick ma'fuckas that think you runnin' shit. You ain't runnin' shit for me! Fuck you!"

Fe-Fe was going off so bad that Teck couldn't get a word in. "Wait a minute, Fe—"

"No, you wait a minute, nigga. Punk bitch-ass, cripple-eyed ma'fucker!"

"Look, I'm sorry, a'ight? Come on. I was buggin'. I should've called, but I didn't."

"Nope." She twisted her lips. "Not workin'! Plus, nigga," she said, reaching under the couch and throwing the jewelry at him, "I'm finding more goddamn goods than drugs. What the fuck is really going on? You robbin' niggas? You a stick-up kid?"

"Hell no!" Teck snapped. "How the hell you just gon' say some shit like that to me? Fuck it, Fe. If it's that deep, fuck it. That's my grandmother's shit. I was hiding it under the couch because I was gon' give it to you."

"Yeah, just like that fuckin' bracelet you embarrassed the shit outta me with! Whatever, nigga. Whatever!"

"A'ight, I see you done got clean and lost your fuckin' mind. Remember I got you out the gutter. You ain't shit but a tramp-ass trash! You just a squirrel try'na get a nut. I made you."

"Look at you, Orange Juice Jones wanna-be ma'fucker! You ain't made me. If anything, I made your no-gamin' ass. If the hustle was left up to you, you'd be in jail for a fuckin' dime piece. You ain't Federal weight yet, nigga. Ya better slow the fuck down, 'fo you get sprayed the fuck down!"

"Sprayed? Oh, now you gon' shoot me?" Teck couldn't help but laugh. He was laughing so hard that before he knew anything, Fe-Fe was laughing.

"Ain't shit funny." She pouted, folding her arms across her breast.

Teck walked over and hugged her. "I'm sorry, Fe, for real. You gotta forgive ya man."

Fe-Fe looked at Teck and couldn't help but to forgive him. She turned around and hugged him. He kissed her and she melted in his arms.

Chapter 7

Constance was in the back seat of her Mercedes, pulling up her satin panties after giving it up to her baby's father, Wallo. They were parked in the bus parking lot behind a few school buses at Selma Middle School. When she was fully dressed, she slid over to him and kissed him deeply for close to five minutes.

"A few more months and we can blow this place," he said, zipping up his jeans.

"I hope so. I'm sick of working at that prison," she said, climbing up to the front seat. "Hey!" she giggled when he squeezed her butt.

He got out and stretched his body then opened her front door to get his helmet. Again, she leaned over to kiss him before he left.

She sat and waited until he got on his Ninja ZX-10R. "I love you," she shouted over the roar of the motorcycle as he revved up the engine before doing a short burnout.

***

Teck came home at 10:38 p.m. to find Fe-Fe wide-awake on the couch, looking at TV. Before she could flip on him, he pulled out a handful of crumpled bills. "I been hustling all day."

"Yeah, right." Fe-Fe sucked her teeth. "Where?"

"In Durham. There's this van that one of my homeboys told me about, and that's where I was. Me and Wallo hopped this van and they took us to a spot to slang."

"Nigga, who is you talkin' to?" Fe-Fe started laughing, "That shit you just said is crazier than a motherfucka. Ain't nobody but five-O promisin' niggas pipe dreams. Like I should believe that a goddamn van gon' take you to slang."

"A'ight, Fe," Teck said, realizing how ridiculous he was sounding. "You got that. I was just doing some things that I don't wanna involve you in . . . but come on, boo," he said, holding her close and kissing her neck. "Anything I do is for me and you."

"I'm pissed at you, boy!"

"Why?" he twisted his face. "'Cause I been out draggin' my ass for you? Other niggas stay out to two or three in the mornin' and some don't even come in at all. And it's what"—He glanced at his watch—"ten forty-five and you trippin'. I coulda stayed wit' some project chick in Durham, but I cut it short and brought my ass home to you!"

***

Anshon was on his knees, leaning forward, braced up on one arm as he used his other arm to hold both of Monica's legs on the right side of his shoulder as he fucked her on her living room floor in front of the TV. Each time he drove into her, it sent her hands to a different part of his body: his neck, shoulders, chest, waist, wrist, ass. Over and over he sought to immerse his entire body inside her.

She had already chanted out his name over a hundred times. It went both ways. He couldn't get enough of her as he switched positions for the fifth time. Her nipples were already sore from his mouth.

"Anshon!"

"Monica!"

They said each other's names as she reached back to spread her ass open for him. The sight of her ass spread with her cheeks apart for him nearly caused him to explode in the condom. He held back and slowly slid back into her pussy.

"Pussy . . . so . . . fuckin' . . . good!" he said through clenched teeth as he watched her butt quiver like Jell-o. The rhythm had her pussy talking as she cried out his name in a feverish lust. Suddenly, they both felt the condom pop.

"Ohhh, baby," he moaned at the sweet feeling of being inside of her raw.

She slowly slid off his dick then pulled the busted condom off. Her lips quivered as he rubbed his throbbing dick against her swollen labia. She fell to her elbows, arching her pussy higher in the air. Anshon flipped her over and placed his mouth back on her breasts as she reached down to mas-sage his dick. She could feel the blood throbbing through his veins.

"Mmmmm, baby," she cried as she crossed her legs over his back and pulled him inside her.

Anshon lost all control as he started pumping her. Monica was talking and mumbling incoherently as Anshon drove deeper into her, causing their sweaty naked bodies to smack together.

She moved his face toward hers for a passionate kiss. Each thrust made him pick up his speed. He came up on his arms, driving deeper, stronger, and harder into her sweet pussy until he exploded deep inside her.

Anshon lost count of the number of times he nutted inside her once the condom broke.

He couldn't believe that he had slipped up and ate pussy till she glazed his face . . . not once, but twice. The only problem was when he was eating her pussy, he kept imaging that it was Fe-Fe's clit he was sucking on. That made him grind his tongue faster, and not until he brought Monica to a triple orgasm did he realize that he'd been totally out of his mind.

After sex, Monica and Anshon rolled over and went to sleep. They didn't wake up until midnight, when Anshon's phone started ringing. He reached over from the bed, hitting the button for the speakerphone.

"Dawg, you up?" It was Teck.

"Um, wassup?" Anshon said with his eyes closed.

"You high or something?"

"Pimp, please. Full night," Anshon muttered, rubbing his neck.

"Yo, I'm about to dip to Goldsboro with Fe-Fe. I'ma take 'er to the movies. She told me you wanted me to call."

"I was tryin' to see what was up with you. Where you bounce to?"

"I was just chillin'. Well, dawg, I'm out. Sound like you in the bed. I'll holla."

As Anshon lay back down, the phone rang again. This time he snatched it off the receiver.

"Speak to a pimp, nigga," Anshon said, flipping his phone open.

"Pimp? Nigga?" Tammy frowned. "Oh, hell no!"

"Big sis!" Anshon sat up in the bed. "Wassup?"

"I met a man, boy."

"For real?" Anshon smiled. "What's his name and address in case I have to bust his ass?"

"Be quiet." She giggled. "His name is Victor. He's a good guy. But look"—Tammy's tone changed from silly to serious—"I hear it's a lotta niggas getting robbed and shit in Selma, Raleigh, and Durham. Even Goldsboro. It's time to give it a rest, Anshon. The South ain't safe no more."

"What is you?" Anshon smirked. "Young Buck? The South ain't safe no more, so what? Get a gun? Well, I got three or four!"

If Tammy could have come through the phone and kick Anshon's ass, she would've. "When are you going to learn that this hustlin' shit is a dead end, huh? You save any money, Anshon? You have any cash in the bank? Or is Monica sportin' every fuckin' name brand in the world? Is the double wide that goddamn laid? Get out the game. Please, it ain't worth it. Look at me. I'm still fighting. I can't even take care of my kids without help."

"Oh, here you go with that bullshit. Tammy, ain't nothin' wrong with you. You met a man, didn't you?"

"Nigga, I met some dick."

"Tammy—"

"No, be quiet, Anshon, and listen. I met a man, but what does that have to do with you being safe? Roll out, Anshon. Ma'fuckers is showin' up dead all over the place. Niggas is gettin' robbed."

"Being robbed don't equal being dead," Anshon snapped.

"Anshon, don't be stupid. All you gotta do is buck and you done."

"Anyway," Anshon said, changing the subject, "how's my niece and nephew?"

Tammy wanted to come through the phone and strangle Anshon. She took a deep breath. "They're fine. Starting to ask questions about their sorry-ass daddy. When I come back to Selma, I may just have to talk to him about seeing his kids."

"Tammy . . ." Anshon swallowed hard.

"What?"

"Tom-Tom . . . is dead."

She dropped the phone, and Anshon could hear her screaming in the background.

"This is what I'm talking about! This is it! What! What! How?" she said, picking the phone back up. "Please don't tell me that you . . . did it!"

"What the hell? Please, Tammy. I'm not answering that."

"I gotta come home." Tammy cried. "I need to see what I can find in my house; maybe some pictures or something for my kids. Maybe I can get by to see his mother. I know she's torn up."

"Tammy." Anshon sighed. "There was a fire."

"What? What does that mean?"

"Your house was burned down. Everybody thinks that Tom-Tom did it."

"I'm on my way," Tammy cried, hanging up the phone.

Anshon hung up with Tammy, took a quick shower, slipped on his jeans, hoodie, and skull cap. He grabbed his heat and car keys.

"Monica." He nudged her a little.

She cracked her eyes open. "Hmm."

"I'll be back later. It's some money on the dresser if you wanna go out. Otherwise, chill here until I come back. A'ight?"

"A'ight, Anshon."

For some reason, Anshon's heart was beating fast as he drove over to Teck and Fe-Fe's. He wondered why Wallo was always missing in action whenever some shit went down, and his mind started to wonder if Wallo was throwing some salt in the game.

And what about Tom-Tom, Anshon thought. *What was that nigga talking about?*

Instead of heading down Lizzie Street, Anshon made a right into Redwood Village apartments to pay Constance a visit. When he pulled up, he saw Wallo's motorcycle parked in her parking spot.

"A'ight." Anshon swallowed hard. "It's all good, 'cause when ya get down to it, pussy is all the same."

He knocked on Constance's door, light at first, until he thought he heard what sounded like fucking sounds coming through the crack of the door. After that, Anshon started kicking the door.

***

Wallo jumped. He was getting his dick sucked, and whoever the visitor was, they'd picked a fucked-up time to come.

"What the fuck?" Wallo said, looking toward the door.

Anshon kicked it again.

Constance unwrapped her lips and wiped her mouth with the back of her hand. Wallo zipped his pants up, but he couldn't erase the attitude off his face.

"What?" Constance snapped at Anshon when she opened the door. "Where's your little seventeen-year-old college groupie?"

"Why you all in my business? What, you wanna suck two dicks? Go find ya kid's father and bust a nut in that nigga's mouth, since you dying to be a ho."

Wallo snatched the door completely open and looked at Anshon. "Yo, Shon." He looked serious. "Don't try and play me crazy. Don't be disrespecting her."

"Oh, my fault," Anshon said, seething. "I ain't know this was your ho now. I thought we was better than that."

"Better than what?" Wallo snapped.

"Than you fuckin' my ex-chicks."

"Yo!" Wallo laughed. "This my daughter's moms. You the one stepped outta line, son. I ain't call you on it 'cause we weren't together. Just like I used to bang Monica, but you ain't need to know that. Not every nigga walking around should be showing his hand. Na'mean?"

"Monica?" Anshon placed his hand on the butt of his gun.

"Chill," Constance pleaded. She knew better than Anshon how much Wallo really hated him. "Just go, Anshon."

"Fuck leavin'." Wallo stepped closer to Anshon. "What you come over here for?"

"Oh, nigga, you really don't want it with me, so you better back the fuck up."

"Whatever," Wallo said, blowing out air.

"Fuck you, nigga," Anshon said, looking Wallo up and down. "I made your crazy-lookin' ass, and you can have the pussy for all the fuck I care. Fuck you. I'ma leave, but don't ever in your life try and punk me, nigga!"

Anshon walked backward to his car so he could leave. He didn't wanna turn his back on Wallo.

When he got in the car, he couldn't believe what had just happened. He called Monica on the phone. "You used to fuck Wallo?"

She was still half asleep. "Wha-what-what? Anshon, please."

"Ain't no *Anshon, please*. Did you fuck Wallo?"

Monica took a deep breath. "We ain't really fuck, Anshon."

"What you mean you ain't really fuck? Either you did or you didn't!"

"Yes, but I was fifteen. That shit don't count."

Anshon hung up on her and drove to Fe-Fe's.

"Yo, Teck," Anshon yelled, rattling Fe-Fe's front door once more.

Dragging herself to the door, Fe-Fe looked at Anshon like he was crazy. "Nigga, it's three a.m. What is your problem?"

"Oh, my fault, shawtie," Anshon said, looking away. Fe-Fe's nipples were hard, and he didn't wanna take his thoughts there. "I needed to holla at my man real quick. It's a lot of niggas gettin' held up and shit around here. Wallo is buggin', and it's just a lot of shit on my mind right now."

Fe-Fe could see the worry in Anshon's face. She let him in and locked the door behind him. "What's wrong?"

Anshon looked at Fe-Fe, and he couldn't help but see how beautiful she was. Her long, black hair was draped over her shoulders.

"You got the kinda hair my sister has." He laughed. "My mother used to put water and lotion in it."

"That's some serious old-school shit, Anshon." Fe-Fe laughed.

"I know." He stood in front of her and ran his fingers through her wavy hair. Immediately her pussy tingled. She backed away and moved slightly so his hand would fall.

"I'm buggin'," he said, moving closer to her.

"I know you are," she said, allowing him to back her against the wall.

"When is Teck coming home?"

"You mean here?" she said, breathing heavy, wanting desperately for him to kiss her.

"Yeah," he said, licking his lips.

"He's not . . . I mean, I don't know. We had a big argument. He said he could set his trap someplace else."

"Oh." Anshon brushed his lips across Fe-Fe's, and she responded by wrapping her arms around his neck.

"Damn, I been wanting to do this for a long time," Anshon said as his hands roamed all over her ass.

"What about Monica?" Fe-Fe asked, feeling Anshon untie her sweatpants.

"She ain't here right now."

"And neither is Teck," Fe-Fe whispered.

"Can I fuck you?" Anshon said, now lifting her shirt above her head. Unsnapping her bra and freeing her breasts, he took a step back.

"What?" she asked, not sure if she should be embarrassed or not.

"You are beautiful."

Before Fe-Fe could respond, Anshon's cell phone started ringing. He looked at the caller ID and saw that it was Monica. He pressed IGNORE and continued to undress Fe-Fe.

"Anshon . . ." Fe-Fe moaned as she lay on the couch, naked and spreading her legs. "This is wrong."

"No, this is all right." He started sucking on her clit. "This feel too fuckin' good to be wrong."

Hours later, Anshon and Fe-Fe had fucked every way imaginable. Anshon lay on the floor and looked at the ceiling, Fe-Fe could tell that he still had a lot on his mind.

"What's wrong, baby?" she said, placing her head against his chest.

"Everything is coming down at once." Anshon turned over on his stomach, and she started to rub his back. "My sister practically cussed me out because she don't want me in the game anymore. Niggas is gettin' robbed all over Selma. Wallo tells me that he used to fuck Monica . . . and she gon' tell me it was when she was fifteen so the shit don't count. What the hell kinda shit is that?"

"Anshon," Fe-Fe said, taking a deep breath, "Monica loves you. Don't hold that against her."

"Yeah, maybe you're right."

"I can't blame Tammy either for wanting you out the game, even though me and Teck making mad money."

"Really?" Anshon frowned. "Teck ain't been to re-up for two weeks. I thought maybe y'all were taking it slow."

"He hasn't been to re-up?" Fe-Fe smirked.

Then she thought, *Maybe he really is selling in Durham.*

"Maybe you should deal wit' Teck on that."

"Oh, best believe I will," Anshon said.

"So, Fe, what's up with all of this?" Anshon asked, turning on his side to feel on her ass again.

"Nothing." Fe-Fe unwrapped Anshon's arms from around her. "Not a thing. We can't let this happen again. As much as I wanna keep fucking you, I can't."

Anshon sat up and reached for his clothes. "Yo, I respect that. I just thank you for being here. I felt like I was going out of my mind. . . . Oh, shit." He snapped his fingers and looked at his watch. It was nine o'clock in the morning. "Tammy! Shit, I forgot that she's coming."

"She is!" Fe-Fe's face lit up. "I can't wait for her to see me clean! Maybe we can be best friends again."

"Slow down, Fe-Fe." Anshon laughed. "Go put some clothes on and then you can come with me to my house and meet her."

"Okay!" Fe-Fe said, laughing on her way upstairs. "I can't wait to see her!"

Anshon ran in Fe-Fe's small bathroom downstairs and showered. As soon as he made sure his pants were straight, he saw Teck standing in the doorway. He jumped.

"Damn, nigga, you scared the shit outta me!" Anshon held his chest.

"It's all good, dawg. Where Fe at?"

"Upstairs."

"Yeah."

"Yeah," Anshon said, giving Teck a pound. "I just stopped by to see if Fe-Fe wanted to ride with me to meet Tammy."

"Tammy?" Teck frowned.

"Yeah, she's coming back in town."

"Oh." Teck thought about the argument he and Fe-Fe had the other night. "Naw, she don't wanna go."

"A'ight," Anshon said, feeling a strange vibe from Teck. He couldn't tell if Teck felt as if some-thing was going on with him and Fe-Fe, or if Teck was just acting funny.

"Fe-Fe, I'll catch you later," Anshon hollered.

Fe-Fe stood at the top of the stairs, out of Teck's sight, and mouthed to Anshon, "Call me."

Anshon nodded his head and then left.

"Come here, Fe-Fe," Teck ordered.

Reluctantly, she walked down the stairs. "What?"

"I'm sorry about the argument we had. You forgive me?"

Fe-Fe rolled her eyes. "Nigga, please. I ain't seen you in a week. You've been disappearing and shit. Humph, and I don't like the way you've been acting lately. Therefore, I don't know who else you been fucking, so—"

"Fe-Fe, please."

"You ain't gotta lie to me, Teck. I don't give a damn. You know what, Teck?" Fe-Fe said, as if an idea had just come to her. "Get your shit and go! Don't come back. The trap is closed."

Teck really wanted to kick Fe-Fe's ass. As far as he was concerned, he'd made her. "Fuck you! Crackhead bitch!"

"Whatever," Fe-Fe huffed. "Come on so I can lock the door behind you, please."

After Teck left, Fe-Fe didn't even drop a tear. She cleaned up her house, took a shower, and lay down to sleep. When she woke up, it was because Monica called her around two o'clock and gave her the good news that she had a job now and that she would start the next week.

Fe-Fe was happy for Monica, but she felt a little sting knowing that her money was running low. Thank God for Section 8 or she would've lost her home a long time ago.

Refusing to fall on her face, Fe-Fe did something she hadn't done in years: She picked up the paper and looked through the classified section. Finding an ad for a bank teller job, she picked up the phone answered the ad. The bank scheduled her an interview for nine o'clock the next morning.

Afterward, she picked up the phone and called her twin sons.

"I wanna see you, Ma," Fe-Fe's son, Jason, said to her. "I miss you and I wanna get to know you. Please, Ma?"

"Yeah, me too," said Jamal, who was on the line as well.

Fe-Fe broke into tears when they asked her if she could talk to their cousin that had legal custody of them. No matter what, they wanted to be with their mother.

"Yes," Fe-Fe said, wiping tears from her eyes. "I'll be up there next week to talk with her."

As Fe-Fe hung up and was wiping her eyes, the phone rang again. It was Monica. Fe-Fe felt guilty about fucking Anshon. She and Monica were so close, but Fe-Fe made herself be at ease, as she convinced herself that she would never sleep with Anshon again.

A few days later, around eight in the evening, it was a full house at Anshon's place. Anshon, Monica, Tammy, Fe-Fe, some of the guys Anshon played ball with—Wood C, Deck, Otis, Don, Tremain—and the two sisters from next door, Dee and Plum, were there. They were playing cards and listening to some old school hip-hop like MC Lyte's "Paper Thin," which was playing at the time.

Tammy was at the table with Don, playing spades against Otis and Tremain.

The small card party they had going on was good for Tammy, because she'd been crying non- stop since she found out that Tom-Tom was dead and her house had burned down.

When she had come to Selma, she wanted Anshon to take her directly to the site of her house, but instead she changed her mind and wanted to place flowers on Tom-Tom's grave. Anshon felt like the Grim Reaper when he stepped foot on Tom-Tom's fresh soil.

He didn't sweat Tammy about the time she wanted to spend at Tom-Tom's grave. The way Anshon saw it, he felt it was better that Tammy be standing over Tom-Tom's grave than Tom-Tom be standing over hers.

Three 40-ounce bottles of Old Gold rested on Anshon's dining room table. In the living room, Anshon sat on the floor next to Monica playing X-Box, as Deck sat between Dee and Plum, knocking down a forty of Old Gold. Fe-Fe sat on the couch, kicking it with Wood C.

"Stop cutting my damn books!" Tammy yelled at Don.

He had a drunk-ass, glassy look in eye. "That wheelchair got hydraulics on it?" He belched. "If not, I could hook ya up. My brother is a bad motherfucker in his two-wheeler!"

Normally Tammy's feelings would've been hurt, but because she knew that Don didn't mean any harm and that he was half drunk, she ignored him. "Shut the hell up and play cards."

Don was so drunk that after a while Dee had to play his hand. Tammy was beatin' Dee's ass. She was running Bostons all over the place. Dee started to get annoyed with Tammy kicking her ass, so she quit the game.

"Sore loser." Tammy laughed.

Fe-Fe was bobbing her head to the music as she peeped Don and Deck creep out behind Plum.

A few minutes later, Anshon asked, "Wood C, where the hell is Deck at?"

"Wit' Plum."

Anshon could only smile. He could only imagine that they were getting ready to run a serious train. And not to be out-done, Dee somehow got Otis and Tremain to follow her next door. She said something about needing a dresser moved. It was quiet, with only Wood C on the couch, along with Fe-Fe and Anshon changing the CDs.

Tammy looked around the room. "Damn, what happen to them cats?"

Fe-Fe laughed. "They next door freakin' Plum and Dee."

Tammy shook her head. "Them girls might as well go into porn."

Don, Deck, Otis, and Tremain didn't come from next door until two hours later. Wood C gave Fe-Fe his cell number then rolled out with Deck.

Otis got behind the wheel of his '79 Cadillac Seville, with Tremain slumped in the passenger seat and Don stretched out in the back. He blew the horn and then rolled out.

"Anshon," Fe-Fe said before she got ready to leave, "I got a job at the bank. I went for my interview yesterday, and they hired me on the spot."

"Get the hell outta here!" He smiled at her.

"Yeah," she said. "My first day is tomorrow."

"That's wassup, Fe-Fe. That's wassup." Anshon kissed Fe-Fe on the cheek before she left. One good thing about Teck was that before he started acting up, he'd bought Fe-Fe a car for her to get around in.

"I'll holla at y'all in the morning. I'm going to bed," Tammy said, heading for the bed.

"Good night, big sis."

Monica closed the bedroom door and started to undress. "I had fun tonight, baby."

"Yeah, me too. My sister's cool, right?"

"Yeah, she is," Monica said, throwing her arm around him. "She really is."

***

Early the next morning Tammy was out and about. Her first mission was to stop at the bank in Raleigh to make a withdrawal to do some serious shopping. She made a withdrawal for $400.00, but a glitch in the system added an extra zero and made it look as if she had withdrawn $400,000. As soon as the teller saw the withdrawal slip, Kristi, Teck's baby mother, nearly broke her neck to call her sister, Constance.

"Constance," Kristi said, breathing heavily, "this is it. We 'bout to strike gold. This chick just made a withdrawal for four hundred grand. Where's Teck and Wallo?"

"I'll call them," Constance said in a hurry.

"They better hurry before she leaves." Kristi looked out the window. "She's driving a white Mercedes truck with a handicap license plate."

"Let me call them now. Damn, Kristi, we struck gold! Maybe I can leave Selma after all."

Kristi turned around smiling, and Fe-Fe was standing there. Fe-Fe couldn't believe what she had just heard. She didn't know who the person was in the white Mercedes, but she knew for a fact that whoever it was, something was getting ready to go down that included this girl Kristi and whoever she was talking to.

Kristi handed Fe-Fe the statement. "Process this," she said.

When Fe-Fe saw Tammy's name, she knew something was wrong. "Oh God, no!" It only took a six-second call to confirm that the computer had made a mistake. Only four hundred was taken out of Tammy's account, not four hundred grand.

Fe-Fe walked over to Kristi's desk, but she wasn't there. Fe-Fe started to panic. She called Tammy on her cell phone, but there was no answer. Then she tried Anshon, and still no answer. Fe-Fe felt like she was going to have a panic attack. Her palms were sweaty, and she was panting. She picked the phone up and called Tammy's cell phone again.

"Hello?" Tammy said.

"Tammy." Fe-Fe was breathing heavily. "Please don't stop and talk—"

"Wait a minute, Fe-Fe," Tammy interrupted her. "It's Te—" The phone went dead.

Fe-Fe took off running out of the bank like a bat outta hell. At that point, she didn't give a damn about her job. Saving Tammy was more important.

Anshon started to worry about his sister when 4:30 p.m. rolled around and she hadn't called. She was supposed to head back to Atlanta that morning, and he knew she wanted to be on time because Q'mara, her daughter, had a school play that Tammy wouldn't dare miss.

For the last hour, Anshon had been dialing Tammy's cell phone non-stop. Then he thought to check his voice mail. Maybe she had called.

He had two messages. The first message was from Tammy.

"Hey, big head. It's your big sis. I want you to know that I love you, and that no matter what, you will always be my heart. I'm heading over to the bank now to take out some money. By the way, I like Monica, but it's kinda obvious that you and Fe-Fe have a thing goin'. Are you tappin' that?"

Anshon smiled. His heart felt content from hearing her voice.

The message continued: "See ya when I see ya."

The second message started to play.

"Anshon," Fe-Fe said, breathing heavily. "Have you seen Tammy? Please get a hold of her. I think someone is trying to set her up."

Anshon felt like his heart stopped. He paced the floor back and forth for two hours. He kept calling Tammy's phone, but there was no answer.

The six o'clock news was just coming on. Monica nervously sat in front of the TV, watching her man pace back and forth.

"Baby," she said as the news continued, "please come sit down. Baby—"

"Monica, be quiet," Anshon snapped. The news broadcast caught his attention.

"This just in," the newscaster said, clearing her throat. "There was a vandalized white Mercedes truck found in the woods of Nashville. An anonymous caller reported this to police. The police are still trying to trace where the call came from. If you have any information on who this vehicle with North Carolina license plate EID987 belongs to, please contact the authorities."

"I gotta go," Anshon said to Monica, grabbing his heat.

"Anshon!" Monica jumped as the phone started to ring. She reached for the phone and snatched it off the receiver.

"What!" she screamed. "You're the police? Yes, we're on the outskirts . . . yes, that's our address."

At the same time that Monica was confirming the address with the police, Fe-Fe was knocking at the door.

"Did you hear from Tammy?" She was hysterical. She took her car keys and clenched them tight. She felt as if she were holding on for dear life.

"No," Anshon said.

Fe-Fe ran into his arms and cried into his chest.

He stroked her hair. "It'll be okay, baby. I promise it will."

Monica was a little taken aback. She was trying to be strong for Anshon, but here he was being strong for Fe-Fe. Seeing her crying in Anshon's arms with him stroking her hair was a bit much. Then she remembered that Fe-Fe and Tammy were the best of friends, so she swallowed what she was feeling for the moment.

When the police came, Anshon and Monica gave them all of Tammy's information and confirmed that it was her truck.

An hour after the police left, Monica looked at her watch. Shit, she was running late for work. She had already missed too many days and was in jeopardy of getting fired. She turned to Anshon, who seemed to catch the way he was holding Fe- Fe, and pushed her away.

"I'ma call out of work," Monica said.

"No, baby, don't. It'll be okay. Tammy will be fine," Anshon said.

Monica turned to Fe-Fe. "Don't let him out of your sight. Please. Do whatever you have to do to keep him here. And call me if something goes down." Monica grabbed her purse and headed out the door.

After Monica left, Anshon felt as if his whole body was in shock. He went into the kitchen and pulled out a bottle of gin and two forty-ounces of Old Gold.

Fe-Fe sat on the couch with tears in her eyes as Anshon sat at the table. After the gin and two forties were gone, he stumbled to the fridge and pulled out two bottles of Mad Dog 20/20.

Fe-Fe started to worry about him. "Anshon, that's enough," Fe-Fe said, standing in front of him. "Please."

He looked at Fe-Fe, pulled her close, and started kissing her. Just then, the phone rang. It was Monica.

"Hello." Fe-Fe answered the phone.

"How is he?" Monica asked.

"Drunk as hell!"

"Maybe I should come home," Monica insisted.

"No, no, stay at work. Everything will be okay."

Fe-Fe hung up the phone. "Let's go sit down, Anshon." She struggled to hold him up, but they fell against the sofa. He started calling out Tammy's name and crying.

"It's gonna be okay," she whispered as she wrapped her arms around him.

He cried out Tammy's name again and then struggled to his feet.

"Gotta . . . go . . . get my sister," he slurred, staggering toward the door.

"No, Anshon!" She grabbed his shirt. "No, Anshon!" She moved in front of him, looking up at him.

He stopped, swayed to the side, then looked Fe- Fe dead in her eyes. "Move. I gotta get my sister."

"No!" She stood her ground, placing one hand on his chest. "I can't let you outta this house, boy. I can't do it. Go sit down!"

"I . . . need my heat." He turned and staggered toward the bedroom.

Fe-Fe knew she couldn't let him get his gun. "Anshon, no!" She ran after him and caught him just as he entered the bedroom.

He was heading for the closest as she tossed her body against him. The beer and wine already had his equilibrium fucked up, so Fe-Fe's body on his back caused them both to tumble on the bed.

Fe-Fe held him down as best she could. Every time he tried to roll out of the bed, she would pull him back by the neck.

"Damn it, Anshon!" she said as he pushed her off, causing her body to roll to the floor, banging the door shut.

Since the hallway light was no longer filling the room, it was now dark. Fe-Fe shot up and jumped right back on his ass as he headed for the closet once more. She grabbed the back of his pants then pulled back with all her might.

When he fell back, he started crying heavily. He wrapped his arms around her.

Fe-Fe knew she had to stay in his arms to keep him calm. Monica's words advising Fe-Fe to do anything to keep Anshon in the house rang in Fe-Fe's ears as Anshon continued to cry.

When he kissed her neck and moved his hands down to her waist, Fe-Fe froze up and pulled away.

"Please don't leave me," he sobbed.

When he rolled over, pinning Fe-Fe on her back, she tried to push him off. He lowered his mouth to hers then kissed her.

Fe-Fe couldn't believe her present situation, in bed with her best friend's man, kissing him as if he belonged to her.

Anshon's hands started to roam under her shirt. He moved from her lips just as his hand reached her soft breast.

"Anshon." Tears filled her eyes as he slid her shirt up. Her lower back arched from the bed as he sloppily started to suck on her breasts. "Nooo!" she whimpered as he started to tug on her pants.

Her mind was saying no, but her hips came up off the bed. She continued to cry as she felt him kiss and lick her now naked body. When she felt his tongue between her legs, she covered her face with her hands and pleaded with him to stop as she opened her legs wider.

***

Two days passed. Tammy still hadn't been found, and Anshon hadn't spoken a single word. He was sitting on the couch, sucking on the tip of a Cuban cigar, thinking about how he should've packed it with hydro, as opposed to leaving the tobacco in it. Monica was leaning against his shoulders, as all of Anshon's boys, with the exception of Teck and Wallo, sat around the living room, waiting to see what their next move should be.

Breaking the silence was a rattling at the screen door. Anshon jumped up, and two detectives were standing there. Anshon invited the detectives in, and everybody stood up, wanting desperately to hear the words that Tammy had been found alive.

Wood C and Deck lowered their heads as one of the detectives started to speak.

"Mr. Green, I'm sorry to have to tell you this, but we were able to identify a body found by Neuse River, near Dunn, as being your sister, Tammy."

Wood C pulled his glasses off, and tears rolled down his face. Anshon stood silently. He was in shock.

The detective continued, "Her body was dismembered, naked, and mutilated. We were able to identify it as being her by her dental records."

Anshon stared at the detectives. His eyes rolled to the back of his head and he passed out.

Monica fell to the floor and cradled his head, trying to revive him. "Come on, baby. Please, come on."

Slowly, Anshon started to open his eyes. "Why she die, Fe? Why?"

Monica wiped his tears. She was too hurt behind Tammy's death and Anshon's reaction to worry about how he'd just called her Fe-Fe's name.

The next day, Tammy's two children and Aunt Rosa, who they were all living with, flew into town. They'd caught the first plane to RDU when Anshon had called to tell them. Aunt Rosa went along with Monica to identify Tammy's body. Anshon couldn't do it. There wasn't a wake held for Tammy due to the condition of her body, and the funeral, held at Howell's Chapel in Selma, was a closed casket.

While the day was bright, Anshon's life was bland and colorless. For his sister, he led a 75-car processional over every inch of asphalt in Smithfield and Selma in his '77 Chevy, with the top down as Jay-Z's instrumental version of "Song Cry" played loudly.

Anshon drove slowly, with the hazard lights on, the system on blast, and the song locked on repeat. In his mind, he was taking his sister on her last ride.

When they rolled through Selma down Preston Street, folks stood on the curb, waving or crying. Kenny-Mac's thirty-deep bike club was acting as the traffic stoppers, and Selma's finest had sense enough to sit their ass on the sidelines and be easy. Niggas were grieving for somebody that didn't need to die.

When Tammy's casket was lowered into the ground, Anshon closed his eyes, and for the first time since he was a child, he said a prayer.

"Now I lay me down to sleep; I pray to the Lord my soul to keep. If I should die before I wake; I pray to the Lord my soul to take." It was the prayer that Tammy had taught him when he was five. She told him that it would fight off the devil.

Anshon pounded his chest so that it wouldn't collapse. He held his nephew Q'shon's hand. The little boy was holding his sister Q'mara's hand.

Anshon said to them, "Uncle Anshon got you. Don't even worry about it."

Anshon's pain was beyond a broken heart and tears. At this moment, he knew that a part of him was dead and there would be no turning back.

He couldn't seem to shake Tammy's conversation with him, when he had begged her to let him deeper into the game. He thought about how she told him, "You can handle your enemies, but you need God to help you with your friends."

At that moment, it clicked. Teck and Wallo had to have their wigs split. Anshon didn't know how or why they had killed Tammy, but something in his heart told him that they had done it. Now it was their time to pay. Fuck forgiveness, fuck letting it slide; someone else besides Tammy had to die.

To Anshon, the world was nothing without his sister. She was his everything.

Chapter 8

Eleven days had passed since Tammy was buried. Everybody else but Anshon was getting on with their lives. Teck and Wallo were nowhere to be found, but Anshon had his hit out.

Fe-Fe continued to work at the bank because Anshon asked her too. He felt she could find out where Teck and Wallo were and how her coworker, Kristi, was involved.

"Anshon, get the door," Monica yelled from the kitchen. She was baking a cake when there was a knock at the front door.

"Wassup?" Anshon said, giving Deck a pound.

"Nothin'. Wanted to know if you wanna shoot some ball today."

"Naw, not today. Kinda hot."

Deck gave him another pound before he turned to leave.

"Anshon, let's go see Q'mara and Q'shon," Monica said, shifting through eleven days' worth of mail that lay on the kitchen table. "Bills . . ." she mumbled to herself, "mo' bills . . . mo' bills . . . Triple Crown . . . another bill. Wait a minute. Triple Crown?" She called out to Anshon. He came and stood in the kitchen doorway, sipping on a cold one.

"Baby, ain't Triple Crown a publishing company?" she asked.

Anshon frowned. "Hell yeah, they're a publishing company. Shit, they write about the shit we live. Tammy used to read their books all the time."

"Well," Monica said, holding the envelope up, "they sent her a letter."

Anshon's face lit up. "Big sis was writing a book." Anshon laughed. "She practically cussed my ass out because I laughed when she told me. Oh, shit! Give me the letter."

Monica handed him the letter and he ripped it open. He read it and looked at Monica. "Baby, they offered Tammy a book deal! They wanna publish her book!"

"All right, baby! All right!" Monica yelled. "See, Anshon, she'll live on. She will."

Anshon called Triple Crown and spoke on behalf of his departed sister. They expressed their sympathy and were happy to be the ones to help keep Tammy's memory alive. For the first time since Tammy had died, Anshon was able to smile.

He stood outside on his patio and tipped his forty-ounce over the ledge. "This one's for you, big sis. *Hood Legend* is gonna be on the streets after all."

Monica went to grab the phone to call and tell his Aunt Rosa the good news. As she picked it up, a woman was already on the line.

"Ah, yes, may I speak to Anshon Green?"

"Who is dis?" Monica asked, wondering who in the hell this woman was calling her man. She looked at the phone and the caller ID was marked private.

Oh, hell naw! Fe-Fe is one thing, but another bitch? Oh, hell no! she thought.

"I'm not at liberty to say that," the woman said.

"Look, bitch!" Monica stood up. "Don't be fuckin' callin' my man, 'cause—"

"Gimme the phone!" Anshon held out his hand. "Yo, who dis?"

"Anshon, we need to talk."

Monica ran to the back room to pick up the phone. It wasn't Fe-Fe, so Anshon didn't care about her picking up the line. As a matter of fact, he didn't start talking until he could hear Monica breathing on the phone.

"I'll talk when I find out who the hell this is!"

"You may not remember me, but this is Larrisha Maynard. We used to date in high school."

"High school? Larrisha Maynard? Don't even play ya self, home girl. Sorry I stood you up for the prom, but goddamn, you should be over it by now. So, Larrisha, I don't know how you got this number, but I'ma kindly ask you not to call here no more."

"Damn straight!" Monica added. "Stank pussy bitch!"

"You the stank pussy bitch, ho!" Larrisha snapped. "And, Anshon, don't flatter yourself. I'm calling because I work here at the bank with Fe-Fe, and she was too upset to tell you what we found out today, so I'm calling to fill you in."

"Speak," Anshon said. Monica was silent.

"I need to talk to you face to face."

"Larrisha—"

"I know who killed your sister." She cut him off.

"I'll meet you at the Burger King on New Bern Avenue at eight. I drive a blue Porsche."

"Yo, what the fuck!" he yelled, but she had already hung up.

When he called Fe-Fe, she was crying so bad that he couldn't understand a word she was saying.

"What's going on?" Monica asked, following Anshon around the house. He went into the living room to search through the phone book for the number to the bank. He tossed the phone on the couch when he was informed that Larrisha Maynard no longer worked at the bank. His temper continued to rise.

So she lied. She just told me that she worked at the bank with Fe-Fe. What the fuck is going on?

"Let's call the police," Monica said softly.

"Hell no!"

"Baby, please don't go see her. What if she's trying to set you up or something?" she pleaded with him.

Anshon wasn't hearing a word Monica was saying. As far as Anshon was concerned, Biggie said it best: "Kick in the door, waving the four-four." Scratch that and fuck a .44. Anshon had a gorilla under the bed: a gold-plated four and a half pound, eight and a half inch barrel, five shot Smith & Wesson fifty-caliber Magnum revolver.

"Monica, listen to me." He turned her face toward him, pointing to the gun.

Monica jumped to the floor. Anshon looked at the gun in his hand and laid it on the bed.

"My fault, baby, but listen, princess. I swear I'm not losing nobody else that's close to me. My momma gone. My sister gone. I never knew my coward-ass daddy. . . . You all a nigga got."

Fe-Fe crossed his mind, but he didn't call out her name.

"Baby, if the wind fuckin' blow hard, I'ma stand in front of you. Don't try to change my mind on this. But if I ever . . . ever find out who took my big sis away from me, I'ma kill 'em."

Anshon picked up his cell and called Wood C and Deck. They agreed to go with him.

Anshon turned to Monica. "I'm leaving."

Monica knew there was nothing she could do. "Please be careful, baby."

"I will. I'm pickin' up Wood C and Deck on my way, and I'll call you as soon as I get there."

She threw a kiss at him through the window, then stood in the front yard to watch him leave.

Since the sun was setting, it was a little dusky as the streetlights slowly came on. Monica wiped her eyes then went to lock the door. A few seconds later, she pulled out in her Nissan.

50 Cent's "I'm Supposed to Die Tonight" filled Anshon's cruising Chevy as he headed toward Raleigh. Anshon made sure he drove the posted speed limit because right now was not a good time to be handing out his license and registration to the police . . . not with his gorilla sitting heavily in his lap.

Wood C was sitting in the front passenger seat, smoking a big head with two Glock .40s under his arms in leather holsters, as Deck sat quietly in the back with a pistol-grip, 32-round clip U.S. Ingram MAC-11.

"Niggas think this is a game," Anshon shouted, pulling into a Burger King parking lot. "They think I'm fuckin' playin'."

Wood C took a pull off his big head. "Niggas think they goin' home, but they're not."

"'Cause they gon be sittin' up in the trunk, startin' to rot," Anshon rapped a little.

Anshon backed into a dark parking spot. It was dark outside, so as Anshon cut the head-lights off, his car faded into the night.

"I'ma go in and order somethin'." Wood C pulled out his twin .40. "These clowns might call the police thinkin' we plottin' to rob the joint."

"Nah," Anshon said, "I'ma go in, just in case she's inside but drove another whip, 'cause I don't see no blue Porsche."

Just as Anshon went to pull the latch on the door, a stunning Carolina blue Audi A8 pulled up and stopped in front of Anshon's Chevy. When the tinted window slid down, Deck simultaneously raised the MAC-11, hoping and praying that whoever was in the Audi tripped.

Wood C and Anshon pressed their bodies against the door in case Deck made up his mind to bust off through the front windshield.

"It's a bitch," Deck said, slowly lowering the MAC-11.

Anshon rose up and saw Larrisha sitting behind the wheel. She had changed a little over the years, but for the most part, she still looked the same. He picked up his .50 and got out. It was hard as hell to hide the gorilla in his pants.

"Where dey at? And how the fuck you know about my sister?" Anshon fired his questions before Larrisha could even get all the way out of the car.

"Anshon . . . we have to sit down and I'll tell you all this from the start. I know you are upset, but please," she said, slightly above a whisper.

"Yo, you don't want it wit' me, kid. For real you don't." He was tempted to pull that gold .50.

Larrisha remained calm. Anshon heard a car pulling up, so he stepped closer to Larrisha, never taking his eyes off her.

"Please, Anshon, follow me back to my house."

"Where's Fe-Fe?" Anshon asked. "I thought you said she knew."

"She does, but she doesn't know everything."

His gut instinct told him not to go, but he needed to find out what Larrisha knew about his sister's death.

Anshon rode with Larrisha to her house, while Wood C and Deck followed behind in his car.

Once inside, Larrisha asked if anyone wanted anything to drink. They all declined. Larrisha sat down and looked at Anshon.

"So, what's up? I ain't come here to flirt," Anshon said sarcastically.

Larrisha crossed her legs, clearing her throat. "I'll start from the very beginning. You already know that I work at the bank—or I used to. Fe-Fe caught the tail end of everything going on, but I was there from the beginning. There's a teller at the bank who I believe is tied up in your sister's murder."

"Who, how, and why?" Anshon asked.

"Please let me explain. Your sister made a four hundred dollar withdrawal, but a glitch in the system said it was four hundred grand. Fe-Fe checked the account and saw that it was wrong. When she left that day in a panic, she dropped the bank slip. I picked it up and checked the account behind her."

"And?"Anshon said, wanting her to hurry up and get to the point. "Fuck all that. Who the fuck killed my big sis?"

Larrisha sighed, uncrossing her legs. "See, I started to notice how after every big withdrawal being made that the teller, Kristi, would leave. And the next day, somebody would end up robbed, shot, or found dead. Well, the day that Tammy came into the bank, Kristi made up a lie about her daughter being sick and needing to leave.

"I know I should not have, but I followed her. First, she went to the Crabtree Valley Mall. I thought I was wasting my time until I saw Kristi park and get into a white Mercedes truck. That's when I started paying close attention. Forty minutes went by, and then she pulled out. I was right behind her, and she never noticed me.

"Five minutes after she pulled out of the parking lot, I noticed that Kristi was making the same turn that a motorcycle was making."

"She was driving my sister's truck." Anshon swallowed hard. His blood pressure was starting to rise. Deck and Wood C remained silent.

"I stayed on Kristi's tail," Larrisha continued, "but I lost her on a back road in Nashville. As I sat waiting for the light to turn green, I noticed her cross back over the street and turn down a dirt road. When the light changed, I followed the skid marks.

"The same guy that was on the motorcycle was waiting there for Kristi. Then Kristi dumped the truck and hopped on the back of the bike. They looked around and then took off.

"When I pulled alongside of the truck, I saw the car registration and driver's license on the front seat. That's when I saw that it was your sister, Tammy, so I called the police with an anonymous tip."

"So it's that bitch Kristi? I'ma kill her! And the bike . . . that's Wallo. I swear to God they're done!" Anshon felt like breaking down crying, but he was determined to hold it together.

"What the fuck you trying to do?" Larrisha snapped. "Go to jail? Just chill for a minute. You can't always show your hand."

Anshon shot her a look. The last time he heard that, it was when Wallo said it. "Go on and finish," he said.

Larrisha took a deep breath. "I don't think it's just Kristi. I believe I know who else is involved, but I need to be sure before I give you a name."

"Why the hell are you telling me all of this?" Anshon clenched his jaw. "Why the hell you ain't tell the police?"

Larrisha looked dead into his eyes. "I have a brother, Anshon. My brother, Von, was in the pool hall that night with Doughnut's baby mother. Doughnut could have killed my brother, so I know if I was in your shoes . . . let's say this: Don't let my feminine looks fool you. I'll kill for my brother and still put my lip gloss on straight."

Anshon's eyes started to fill up with tears. Larrisha knew that his pain was hurting him deep. She felt like crying herself.

Anshon realized that his sister was tortured for money she didn't have. Tears rolled down his face. His vision blurred as Deck and Wood C stood there trying not to cry.

"Yo," Wood C spoke for the first time. "How you livin' so large? I know these cribs out here cost 'bout three hundred Gs or more. And my man said you had a Boxter and now you pushin' an Audi. Your clown-ass brother ridin' in a Volvo with spinners. How we know you ain't followin' peeps and doin' your thang? Answer that."

Anshon wiped his eyes then glared at Larrisha. Wood C was dead on the money.

Larrisha ignored the remark about her brother as she reached for her Marc Jacobs tote bag from the floor. She opened it then pulled out a business card and handed it to Wood C.

L&K Investment Consultants
We Research, Observe, Borrow,
Keep Investments Limited and Legit
Ms. L. Maynard and Ms. K. Batts

Larrisha allowed him a few seconds to study the card before she explained the legal hustle she ran with her brother. Wood C looked up.

"We research the stock market, New York Stock Exchange," Larrisha continued, "the Amex and Nasdaq to find the hot commodities or a company that will soon be in a real high demand. We then observe the buying trend of that market, and if it looks good, we borrow money to buy shares or make an investment. Our motto is to keep investments limited. That way we never take a big loss if things flop, and of course"—She smiled—"we keep all our business legit."

Larrisha pulled the diamond pin from her hair then explained to Anshon how she had a plan that she felt would work . . . a plan that her brother didn't agree with, but she didn't care.

Anshon was all ears. All he wanted was a name, but for now, he'd play her game.

Anshon, Wood C, and Deck made it back to Selma before twelve that night. Monica was in the bed asleep, but she quickly woke up.

"Anshon, baby, what's going on?"

He gave her the short version, leaving out some details on purpose. Then he took off his clothes, showered, and changed.

"Deck and Wood C in the living room waiting on me," he said before leaving again. "We gon' run by Ms. Johnnie Ray's shot house. I promise I'll be back by three."

Monica didn't really want him to go, but she felt that she had no choice. "Okay, baby."

Anshon took the back seat in Wood C's 300C as they headed to get their drink on. When they pulled up, they found the spot packed. The twins saw Wood C's 300C and waved him over to park behind their chromed-out minivans.

"'Sup, dawg? E'rythang straight?" Teck said, giving them some dap. Wallo followed his brother's lead.

"Look, Anshon," Wallo said, "I know we had some words the other day, but it's all good. We still peoples and shit. I'm sorry to hear about Tammy. I just found out. I was down in Murfreesboro. My aunt died."

Anshon nodded his head to make them think that everything was straight.

"A'ight," Teck said. "First round on me."

"Y'all just gettin' here?" Anshon asked, going up the stone steps.

"Yeah. Fid'na get tipsy then find somethin' to smash," Teck replied.

Inside the 1930s-built house, the music was blasting, and a thick haze of smoke filled the living room. Big-titty Gale was solo dancing on the worn-out carpet with a glass of gin in one hand and a cup of O.J. in the other. Al Green's music was helping her to get her groove on.

In the kitchen, two old heads were beefing at each other over a dominos game, while Fernistein stood at the gas stove frying chicken. Teck and Wallo had stopped cooking food in the yard, so Ms. Johnnie Ray started selling food again.

Staying true to his word, Teck pulled out his knot and hit Freddy off to pay for the first rounds of brew. Freddy ran the liquor spot with Ms. Johnnie Ray, along with a short temper and an even shorter sawed-off pistol-grip pump.

On the low, this spot was a brothel, so Freddy and Ms. Johnnie Ray could also be held liable as pimps. They had two Mexicans from Smithfield that were far from attractive, but that was okay, because it was pussy they were selling.

The taller one with the black hair signaled Wallo out and talked him into following her to the back. Teck shook his head then turned to Anshon, Wood C, and Deck.

"Why you in such a good mood?" Anshon shouted to Teck over Al Green playing in the background.

"You ain't heard?" Teck moved in closer. "I beat the McMillan basketball team today!"

"Yeah, right," Wood C replied, leaning on the freezer.

"Word, dawg," Teck proclaimed.

"Who was all out there?" Anshon asked, finding it hard to believe.

Teck held a finger up as he downed his cup of gin. "Whew!" He pounded his chest, as the gin caused a burning sensation. "Shit like moonshine! But anyway, Markie was out there . . . Clevan, Kayo, Varis, Fonz and his brother, and some herbs from Micro."

"What was the score?" Anshon asked before he sipped his gin and juice.

"We won by one. Twenty-one to twenty," Teck bragged. He then went on to tell them about Janis out in Johnston Court in Smithfield. She was having a welcome home party for her sister, who had pulled a five-year bid. They all wondered who would be the lucky man to bust that pussy wide open.

Deck finished with the Latin whore in the back and then excused himself to go make a call. He dipped out to the front yard to use his cell phone and called Don. His 14-year-old sister, Fatima, picked up on the sixth ring.

"Who dis?" Fatima asked.

"Don in?" Deck asked.

"Nope."

"Where he at?"

"I'on't know. He left on a motorcycle about an hour ago."

"Who bike he on?"

"I'on't know, boy. Ain't keepin' tabs on him."

"A'ight. Just tell 'im to call me and to bring my clippers next time he come by my crib."

"Okay, bald head." She giggled before she hung up.

Deck flipped his phone closed then headed back inside. In the corner, he saw Anshon and Teck in a deep conversation. Wood C was tripping out with Gale, dancing and sipping on gin. Every new song that came on, she would raise an arm in the air and shout, "Dat's my shit!"

The scene kinda took Deck back to the good old days. Club 82, back in 1994 . . . man, he missed those days. If there was beef, it was settled with the hands, but now it was all about the chrome or metal.

He went up to Freddy and bought a cup of gin with no chaser, then posted up against the freezer to watch Wood C get his clown on.

Anshon moved from the corner to sit on a stool as Teck went to take a piss. He yelled out for Freddy to fill one up for him with a squirt of juice. He spun around on the stool to come face to face with the second Mexican chick.

"You wanna go talk?" she said with a slight accent.

"Nah, I'm good, senorita," he said, turning her down.

"Are you sure? I bet I can suck your dick all the way down my throat."

"No haps on this one."

She said something under her breath in Spanish then stepped off. Freddy handed him his drink a few seconds later. This would be his last round.

He later joined Wood C, Teck, and some dude from Kenly at the dominos table. He was feeling good as hell.

Wallo was getting his major trick action on with the Mexican. First he had her snort a line of powder off the length of his erect dick, then had her suck him off. He got souped up then rolled on a jimmy and fucked her doggy style in the back bedroom. He spanked her and told her to call him Daddy. After he paid for her services, he went to the bathroom and walked in on big-titty Gale.

"Boy!" she shouted. "You see me in here. Get the fuck out!"

Deck was done with the gin. It was time to get his smoke on. Oh yeah, Freddy also sold some phat joints, and the weed was straight! Freddy stayed busy as Deck asked him for some hot sauce for his chicken.

"A nigga feeling good tonight," he joked.

About six or seven minutes later, Wallo exited the bathroom. Taking a large bite from his greasy chicken, Deck went to empty his bladder. From across the room, Teck yelled out that he was on his last domino.

Deck staggered into the bathroom and kicked the door closed behind him. He was halfway finished pissing when he heard someone cough behind him. He nearly pissed on his jeans as he reached for his .32. The cough came from behind the dingy shower curtain. Deck opened it with the stubby barrel of his .32. only to find Gale curled up in the tub with a bloody mouth. Deck used to kick it with her niece back in the days, and Gale had once hid him in the closet when his P.O. was looking for him. So, he felt close to her. He put up his .32 then reached down to help Gale out of the tub.

"What the hell you doin', Gale?"

"One of dem twins tried to make me suck his dick," she murmured.

"Say what!"

"Don't cause no trouble, Deck," she pleaded as Deck helped her stand up.

"Did he hit you?"

"Yeah . . . but it ain't nothing. I'ma be fine."

"Look," Deck said, reaching for a towel. "Clean yourself up and go home."

She pushed the towel away with a frown on her face. "Get dat nasty thing outta my face. Dem Mexicans might be using dat to wipe their funky tails."

Deck saw that she was fine, just had a small cut on her lip. Leaving her, he went back into the living room to find Anshon, Wood C, and Teck getting up from the dominos table. He searched for Wallo and found him standing by the door, feeling up on the second Mexican.

Deck approached the group just as Teck was telling Anshon and Wood C that they should roll with them to Johnston Court. Wallo walked over to his brother's side. Deck was waiting for an opening in the conversation; then he played his part.

"Y'all hear about Robert?" Deck asked the group.

"Nah, what up?" Teck asked.

"Man, that lame-ass coward got locked up for beatin' on his girl. Said he broke her arm or some shit."

"Word?" Anshon replied.

"Yeah," Deck continued with his eyes locked on Wallo. "To me, a nigga is a straight bitch if he hits a woman."

"Fuck you mean-muggin' me fo'?" Wallo said, returning Deck's glare.

"'Cause you's a lame-ass nigga. That's why!"

"Hold up, Deck!" Anshon put his hand on Deck's chest. He looked at Deck like he was crazy. Hell, he was fuckin' up the plan they had.

"Yeah, hold up, nigga!" Teck jumped in. "You got beef with my brother?"

"Fuck you and your coward, bitch-ass brother, nigga!" Deck snapped.

"Say what!" Teck reached under his Zoo York shirt. Wallo did the same, but they were slow to the punch, as Wood C had his two .40s aimed at their chests.

"What the fuck?" Anshon shouted as he tried to calm things down. "Deck, what's up?"

Wood C kept his two pistols aimed at the twins, while Deck told Anshon what Big Gale had just laid on him. Anshon nodded his head.

"Wood C, put the heat up." He turned to Teck and Wallo. "Y'all need to roll out. I'll call you tomorrow, Teck," Anshon said as the twins walked toward their new Nissan minivans.

"Yeah, dawg," Teck shouted over his shoulder. "And you betta let Deck and Wood C know wassup. We got guns too. I'ma let this shit ride, but a nigga come at me or my brother sideways again ain't gonna be no talkin'. Nigga betta keep ya third eye peeled open."

"Don't be makin' no threats on my fam," Anshon warned him.

Teck sucked his teeth. "Fuck you! You better be easy, nigga, 'cause you could get it too. Matter of fact, fuck all you bitches. Y'all can suck my dick!"

"You got a lot of mouth," Anshon snapped.

"You don't put fear in my heart. Nigga, you must got me mixed up with Tom-Tom."

"Let it go, Teck," Anshon said.

"Come to Durham and get put to sleep, cowards. You betta recognize."

"Teck!" Wallo called out to his brother. "Fuck all this lip-boxin'. Let's roll on them niggas. They know where we live at. Fuck 'em."

As the twins drove off, Wood C moved beside Anshon and Deck.

"You know we got beef with them clowns," Wood C said, pulling out a Newport. "What was that Tom-Tom remark about?" Wood C asked.

Anshon played it off by shrugging his shoulders. "Check this," Anshon said. "Them clowns even bend a blade of grass in my yard, I'll kill 'em. Yo, take me home. I'm done for tonight."

***

Early the next morning, Constance was at the Super 8 Motel in Smithfield with Wallo. She was on her elbows and knees as he drilled her from the back. Sweat coated her naked body as their moans filled the dark room. Her ass was jiggling like jelly as his hips smacked into her ass over and over. She clutched the pillow in her hands as her pussy started to tingle. She loved to get fucked this way.

"Harder!" she shouted over her shoulder then threw her left hand back to place it on his sweaty stomach. She felt him grip her waist tighter, pulling her back against his strokes. She arched her ass higher in the air and started breathing through her mouth. "I'm gonna cummmm!" she moaned.

At the same time in the room next door, Kristi sat on the bed beside Teck, watching TV. It was the first time she'd seen him since Tammy's murder.

"What's wrong wit' you?" Teck asked.

"Nothing," she mumbled. "Just had a long day, that's all."

"Yeah, right." He frowned. "You still think we holdin' out on the money, huh? I told you she didn't have shit on her."

"Look." She looked at him. " I saw the bank statement myself! I know she had the money . . .

but she didn't have to die for it. Did you let her see your face or something?"

"Yeah, and she saw my tattoo. Plus she called my name and accused me of shooting her the first time."

"Well, you did!"

"So the fuck what! That's why I had to do her in this time. I know she would've told."

"Goddamn, Teck!" Kristi screamed. "We made a deal that nobody would get killed. That's what the masks are for. Goddamn, first the robbery in the club that night got fucked up by Doughnut, and now this!"

"Fuck all that," Teck said. "We wouldn't be so behind if you hadn't fucked up most of the $287,000 we robbed Tammy of from the first heist!"

Kristi rolled her eyes. "That still isn't an excuse to kill."

"Like you got a damn conscience now. You driving a Lex with blood money."

"This is a bunch of crap," she huffed. "Whatchu say!"

"Nothing. Just drop the issue."

He switched the TV off and told her to shut up and undress. Reluctantly, she did as he asked.

Back in Constance's room, she was having the same conversation with Wallo, and she, too, wanted to know why they had killed Tammy. She just couldn't understand it, especially after the way shit backfired with Doughnut. Plus, she didn't receive her usual cut and was tired of all this robbing with nothing to show for it. Sure, she had a new Benz, but she was still struggling to make ends meet.

At first things were okay, but then they started to get out of hand. Now she felt like they were robbing for anything. Now they were making licks for something as petty as five grand. Constance was starting to get a bad feeling about the entire setup. Sure, she loved Wallo and had a baby with him, but she would quickly draw the line when it came to going to prison because of him. Ride or die was not on her mind. She knew how Anshon felt about his sister, and she had lost a lot of respect for her man behind Tammy's death.

Kristi was now afraid of Teck, and her building fear pushed her toward betrayal. She loved him, but not that much. She agreed with anything he said to avoid beef. She was relieved when he got tired of her attitude and left.

She got out of bed and went to her sister's room. Wallo had just left out on his motorcycle. Now Kristi and Constance were alone and scared. They quickly devised a plan to make sure they wouldn't go down when the shit hit the fan.

***

Monica surprised Anshon when he got home. He was in the bathroom brushing his teeth when she came in with her birth control pills in her hand. He watched her flush them down the toilet.

"Anshon, I want a baby," she said with tears in her eyes.

It was a subject they had already spoken on, and Anshon was with it. They made love in the bathroom then moved to their bedroom. Each stroke, he told her how much he loved her and that she was the only woman for him. Although he had to keep pushing thoughts of Fe-Fe out of his mind, he was serious about what he told Monica.

Her nails dug into his waist as she clung to him. Monica was madly in love with Anshon and would do anything for him. She was whole-heartedly committed to him.

Earlier when Anshon was in Raleigh with Wood C and Deck, she drove to a gun shop in Benson and bought a pump that was now under the bed. She'd kill for her man, and when he planted his seed deep inside her, she cried out his name while her pussy exploded with pleasure.

***

Fe-Fe slid out of bed, trying to shake thoughts of Anshon from her mind. She tipped down the hall and peeked into the bedroom she'd fixed up for her sons. Her cousin had agreed to let them come and stay with her for a while. Fe-Fe couldn't wait.

As she walked on the cold floor, she felt a chill go up her spine. She'd been sick for a little over a week now, and her breasts had been sore for a while. She reached in her bathroom cabinet and pulled out a pregnancy test kit she had purchased at Wal-Mart.

This was actually the second test she'd bought this week. The first test she took, she swore the results were wrong. Being that she was feeling better, she thought she'd try it again. She pissed on the tab then waited for the sign.

"Damn!" she muttered a few minutes later. It was just like the first one. "Fendisha Lloyd," she said to herself, "how the hell did you let this happen?"

Right away, there was no question of who the child's father was. The only problem would be telling him.

Chapter 9

Anshon woke up with a lot on his mind. He was thinking about Larrisha and if she could really lead him to the muthafuckers that took his sister's life. He had no doubt in his mind that he would kill again, but he had to control his temper or else Monica would be paying him visits in the Central Prison, and that was not what he wanted.

He remained still about an hour and then slowly he slid the covers down Monica's waist until her soft, bodacious brown ass was fully exposed. He licked his fingers then raised his hand and brought it down hard.

Monica woke up screaming and rubbing her stinging butt cheek as Anshon rolled out of bed before she could retaliate.

"Boy!" she shouted. "That shit hurt. I'ma get your ass!" She kicked the covers off and jumped out of the bed, tits and ass bouncing everywhere, and it was a lovely sight to see.

Since he had a head start on her, he was able to slam and lock the bathroom door in her face.

"Be out in a sec!" he shouted through the door, laughing as she pounded on the door. "Dat ass hot, ain't it?" He laughed.

"You can't stay in there all day!"

"Yeah, yeah, yeah. I'll holla at ya later, princess." He flipped the lid on the toilet and took a long, relaxing piss that made him tingle and twitch at the end.

"Open the door," she pleaded. "I gotta pee."

"Hol' up, shawtie."

"For real! I gotta pee real bad!" she pleaded.

"If I let you in . . . can I look?" he asked.

"Look at what?"

"Look at you pee."

"Boy, I don't care."

"A'ight, but don't cut one loose up in here." He laughed. He was still butt-ass naked when he unlocked the door and opened it. There stood his thick-ass girl, naked, with a smile on her face and a plastic cup of ice cold water.

"Aaaaaaaargh!" Anshon yelled as Monica doused his ass. He cringed as the cold water shocked him from head to toe. "That shit was cold!" he said through clenched teeth.

Monica burst out with laughter as the empty cup fell from her hands. She was still laughing as she pushed past him to take a piss after flipping the seat back.

"We even now?" Monica said as she finished using the bathroom.

"Yeah," he said, rubbing his ass. "I'm jumpin' in the shower."

Monica waited until he closed the curtain and turned the water on before she flushed the toilet.

"Slide over, Bookie," she said, joining him in the shower. They took turns cleaning each other from head to toe.

"French toast or pancakes?" she asked, wringing her rag out as Anshon stood under the shower. She liked to look at his naked muscular body that turned her on with ease and took care of her needs 24/7.

"Pancakes," he said, wiping water from his eyes.

"Um . . . bacon or sausage?"

"Both."

"Boy, make up your mind!" she said, popping his ass with the rag. She reached out and rubbed the spot before he could do it himself. "That better?"

"Yes." He nodded, still wiping water from his face. "I'll take bacon." He made his mind up.

She already knew the rest—scrambled cheese eggs, grits with breakfast sausage from the can, and toast.

"Monica." His body glistened from the creamy baby oil Monica had rubbed on him as they stood in the middle of the bathroom.

"Um, what?"

"I love you," he said, caressing her oily breasts.

"I love you more, Bookie."

As they ate breakfast, the temperature outside was creeping up to eighty-nine degrees.

"What's up for today?" Monica asked, lounging on the sofa in a pair of Triple S high school gym shorts and a tank top.

"We can work on the baby all day," he said, crunching on a piece of bacon.

"Now that sounds like a good idea. But I'm on top first." Monica laughed as the phone rang. She reached across him, picked it up, and handed it directly to Anshon. It was Wood C.

"Holla."

"Yo," Wood C said, "I ran into the twins at the Waffle House last night."

"What happened?" Anshon moved to the sofa.

"Teck was there, and he wanted to shake on the beef. He wanted it squashed."

"Word?" Anshon was surprised because Teck wasn't known to cop a plea.

"Yeah. We went to check on Lori's party. He told me to call you and try to let the shit die. He said y'all go way back and that Wallo was in the wrong. You know how shit be."

"What about Deck?"

"Called him over the phone."

"Good. That's less stress I gotta worry about."

"I feel ya. But yo," Wood C said, "let me know the deal 'bout what ol' girl Larrisha say. You know I'm wit'cha on layin' down whoever—"

"Yeah, I gotcha," Anshon said, cutting him off. The thought of Tammy made him wanna cry. "Biggie said it best," he added.

"Somebody gots ta die!" they said simultaneously.

"Anshon," Monica said when she saw him press the END button on the phone.

"Yeah?"

"Would you . . . really kill somebody?"

Anshon laid the phone on the table. "Don't ask me nothing like that, princess."

She lowered her head. "I wish none of this had happened. What if something go wrong and you end up in prison?"

"Princess—"

"Wait." She looked at him. "What about me, Anshon? I know you loved your sister . . . but we both know how she felt about you going back to prison. That night we went out to get some beer, she was telling me to not let you stay in the game."

"Monica, have I been selling anything since Tammy died?"

"No."

"A'ight then, case closed."

She reached out to touch his shoulder. "Baby, I don't wanna see you go to prison."

"Shut the fuck up!" he exploded. "She wasn't your goddamn sister!"

Before Monica could calm Anshon down, he had thrown on his clothes, snatched his keys off the table, and headed for the door.

"Anshon, wait!" Monica shouted, running to the door. When she grabbed his shirt, he turned and twisted from her grip. "Baby, please don't leave!" Tears filled her eyes as she stood on the porch, watching him get into his car. "Anshon!" she pleaded as he rolled out the driveway.

Anshon didn't make it back home until 9:30 p.m. He'd been riding around for hours. He felt bad leaving Monica the way he had, and he knew he needed to go back home and apologize.

As soon as he opened the door, he paused at the sight of countless burning candles. All of the furniture was moved into the kitchen. He closed the door. When his eyes adjusted to the dim lit setting, he saw several pillows and silk sheets in the middle of the floor. Just as he was about to call Monica's name, Kem's "Love Calls" came from the back room, followed seconds later by Monica appearing in the hallway.

Anshon was speechless as she walked toward him. Her skin was glowing with oil, and her sexy brown body was covered with a purple J-Lo lace thong and a sheer matching corset. Her cleavage was big enough to catch and seduce Anshon's eyes with ease. On her feet were a pair of purple stilettos. His hard dick beat his mouth to the apology he owed her.

"Shhhh." She started to undress him. "Don't you ever in your life leave me again, Anshon." She pulled his shirt off and made him step out of his pants. "Tonight, we ain't gonna do no talking. I'ma show and prove my love, not lust, but love for you." She pulled him to the floor and let nature take its course.

Fe-Fe was surprised when Teck showed up at her front door. She hadn't seen him since last month, nor had she wasted her time in calling his ass. She was home alone, dressed in nothing but her Champion T-shirt.

"What's up?" she asked, letting him in.

"Just thought I'd swing by to see how you doin'," he said, looking at her bare legs. He knew she probably sported some panties under that shirt. "Got company?" he asked.

"Fool, you think I'd let your ass in if I had company?"

"Shit, you walking around in your T-shirt with no panties on." He grinned, flipping the hem of her shirt up.

"'Cause it's my damn house! Even if it is a fifty-dollar-a-month Section Eight spot. The shit is mine!" She flicked the lights on.

"What happened to your tattoo? The eagle on your shoulder?" She pointed to his bare arms. He was wearing a wife beater.

"I had it removed."

She looked at him again, and for a moment, she could've sworn that he was Wallo. Wallo and Teck may have been identical twins, but most people could tell them apart by the way they acted, but right at this moment, Fe-Fe didn't know the difference.

"Damn . . . why you lookin' at me all crooked?" he asked.

"Do you see what time it is?" She folded her arms.

He glanced at his watch. "It's 11:15 p.m. Oh, you got a bed time?"

"Look, I ain't stayin' up all damn night. What do you want?"

"I just wanna see you." He stepped toward her, but she stopped him with a stiff arm.

"It ain't like that no more," she snapped.

"C'mon, baby." He reached for her thigh.

"I said no!" She pushed his hand away. She hoped he wouldn't notice her nipples getting hard.

"Fe-Fe, damn," he protested. "I really been thinkin' about you."

"Nigga, please!" she exclaimed. "You need to be missin' the freaks you got in Durham, so don't come at me with that lame game."

"You think I'm runnin' game? Word on my life I wanna get back wit' you."

She laughed in his face. "Who you think you foolin'?"

He took a glance and slid closer. "Fe-Fe, I'm the deal real. What I gotta do to prove it? Fuck them freaks in Durham."

"Teck, you come on a booty call and talkin' 'bout you wanna be with me. All you want is the bomb pussy. You don't give a damn about me."

"Listen, baby, believe me. I know I fucked up and let the paper get to my head, but I got on my feet because of you, baby. I want to make it like it used to be. You and me, fuck everything else.

Let a nigga prove it." He moved his hand to her warm, soft thigh and grinned at the two imprints of her nipples.

Fe-Fe looked into his eyes as he slid his hand higher up her thigh. When he moved closer, she moved away from him until her back touched the arm of the couch. She felt his fingers rub against her pussy lips. She opened her legs. Then she changed her mind.

"No, Teck, no!" Tammy's death flashed into her mind. In Fe-Fe's heart, she felt like Teck and Wallo had something to do with Tammy's death.

"You fuckin' bitch!"

Chapter 10

"Anshon, phone!" Wood C shouted from the kitchen.

"Speak," Anshon said when Wood C handed him the phone.

"This Anshon?" a soft voice asked.

"Yeah, who dis?"

"This is Larrisha."

"Look, your plan is taking too fuckin' long. You got somethin' or not?"

"Yes. I have a name."

"What is it?"

"Kristi. Kristi Connelly. She drives a gold Lexus." She gave Anshon Kristi's license plate and address. "Her sister's name is Constance Connelly. She's a prison guard. The ball is now in your court."

As Anshon stormed out the door to his Chevy with Deck and Wood C on his heels, he could only think of revenge for his sister.

They stopped in Clayton first. Deck picked up his MAC-11, then the three moved on to Cary.

Wood C had two glocks, and Anshon had his gorilla back in his lap.

"Stay within the speed limit," Wood C cautioned as Anshon became heavy on the gas. "We don't need to get caught behind no bullshit."

Once they reached Cary, it took them close to thirty minutes to find Kristi's place, and just as Larrisha promised, a gold Lexus E330 was sitting in the parking lot.

Kristi was in the kitchen talking to her sister, Constance, and making plans to tell Anshon the truth about Wallo and Teck.

Anshon knocked on the door. "Who is it?" Kristi asked politely.

"Somebody order pizza?" asked the voice from behind the closed door.

"Let me call you back, Constance." After hanging up the phone, she looked through the peephole to see who she thought was a pizza deliveryman with his back turned.

They're always getting the duplex numbers wrong, she thought.

Kristi opened the door, and before she could say a word, two masked men forced their way in. Wood C backed up and tossed the empty pizza box he had found in the dumpster to the floor, as he pulled his mask down.

Deck went to search the rooms with the MAC-11, as Wood C took up his spot by the window. Anshon had the gorilla pointed at Kristi's head, as Deck cased the place to make sure she was alone.

"Now," Anshon said from behind the masked face. "I want some fuckin' answers, Kristi Connelly, and I want the right ones!" He pointed a black gloved finger at her.

Kristi was cringed up on her sofa with her eyes locked on the big gun stuck in her face.

"Now, question number one," Anshon said. "Where do you work?"

"At . . . a bank," she said, trembling.

"Is Constance your sister?"

"Yes," she cried.

"Tell me what happened when the young lady in the white Mercedes truck was killed."

"I don't recall." She shrugged her shoulders.

Anshon cocked the hammer back, making the five-shot chamber slowly rotate. The loud click made tears fall from her eyes. Kristi buried her face in her hands.

"Bitch, you got Alzheimer's or somethin'? Now let's try this again." He yanked her up by her hair and placed the barrel to her head.

"Please!" she sobbed. "Oh God, p-please don't kill me."

"Don't kill you? Do you think the woman in the Mercedes truck begged for her life? Now

shut up!" he shouted. "And answer my fuckin'
question!" His voice was laced with anger.

Kristi slumped to the floor as he shoved her to
the ground.

"Answer the question!"

"I went to work," she cried, "at the b-bank that
day."

"And!"

"I . . . left w-w-work early."

"Go on!"

"I called my baby's father."

"Teck?"

"Yes."

"And what?" Anshon said through clenched
teeth.

Tears slowly fell from Kristi's eyes as she came
clean. "It was Teck and Wallo. Not me . . . or my
sister. I swear to God it wasn't us."

"Bitch, if you wanna live, you better give me the
right answer!" Anshon said with the gun back to
her head. "Did dem clowns rob my sister?"

"Yo!" Wood C exclaimed, but it was too late.
Anshon had slipped up and gave a clue to who
he was.

"Anshon, please," Kristi cried.

"Man, shit!" Deck cursed. They knew what
had to be done.

"Please don't kill me," she cried on her knees.
"I didn't know they were gonna kill your sister. I
was gonna call you anyway . . . me and my sister."

"Let's go see them niggas!" Wood C said. "Fuck all this talk!"

Anshon took a deep breath to slow his heartbeat down. He glanced at Deck. Deck nodded his head.

"Please don't kill me, Anshon," she pleaded. "Please, oh God," she cried.

He slowly backed up, and she ran toward him.

"Slow the fuck down!" Wood C came up from behind, grabbed her chin, and placed a hand on her forehead, snapping her neck. Her body jerked around on the floor for a few seconds before she dropped dead.

A few minutes later, they were back in the Chevy with Wood C behind the wheel. "Which twin we gettin' first?" Wood C asked.

Anshon shrugged his shoulders with tears running down his face. "My sister told me," he sniffed, "that you can take care of your enemies, but you need God to help you with your friends. She ain't never lied."

"Let's do this shit right, y'all!" Wood C said. "Let's lay these clowns down on the low so we can still walk da streets. I ain't goin' to prison and ain't gonna go on the run, so let's think this shit through, a'ight?"

"No doubt!" Deck added from the back.

***

Wallo, who was still pretending to be Teck, woke up with a broken glass bottle to his throat. Fe-Fe looked him in the eyes. "I done been on the streets long enough to let a nigga know that I ain't the one. If I say don't fuckin touch me, don't fuckin' touch me."

Wallo looked at Fe-Fe like she was crazy. "You got that, ma. You got that."

The real Teck was in Redwood with Constance. He stood in her kitchen with Wallo's motorcycle helmet in his hand as Constance tried to call her sister Kristi for the third time.

"I don't understand why she's not picking up the phone," Constance said.

"Try your momma's crib," Teck suggested.

"I know she's not there."

Teck glanced at his watch. "Find that bitch!" he spat. "And you better know where she is by the time I get back!"

Constance just wanted Teck to leave so she and Kristi could carry out the plan to tell Anshon about Teck and Wallo.

"Where you going?" Constance asked.

"Back to the storage to get my ride and park his."

"Why y'all switch?" Constance pressed.

"Does it matter?" he said, putting the helmet on. Teck knew his brother was over at Fe-Fe's.

The original plan was for Teck to kill Constance because she was beginning to talk too much.

When she had first started fucking with Anshon in prison, the plan was for her to find out where Anshon and Tammy kept their work and their stash; but for some reason, Anshon didn't let Constance get too close to him.

Constance figured she'd take a shower before she headed to Cary. She tried calling Kristi but was receiving no answer. Constance stepped out of the shower ten minutes later. She wrapped the towel over her breasts and tiptoed into her bedroom. She nearly slipped and fell on her ass when she found Anshon sitting on her bed.

"How did you get in here?" she asked. "Better yet . . . why are you here?"

"The door was opened up when I knocked," he lied. He had come through the back door by picking the lock after creeping through the woods. "Me and my girl got into a fight.".

"Oh." Constance smiled. "Well, in that case." She took the towel off and walked toward him. She made her breasts jiggle from side to side.

"So you miss me, huh?" She reached for his hand, placing it between her legs.

"Wallo ain't gonna show?"

"No, baby. He's in High Point." She sat next to him and went to work at his zipper. "Baby, I miss this so much," she purred, pulling his dick out and playing with it.

He didn't say anything as she buried her face in his lap and started sucking his dick. He was kind enough to hold her wet hair.

She really got into it, bobbing up and down with quick motions. "Mmmmmm!" she moaned as she took him deeper into her wet mouth, making him cum with the last stroke of her tongue.

"Drink that cum, baby," he moaned as she lapped it up. "That's it." He stroked her hair. "All of it."

Once she was done and lifted her head up to ask if he had a condom so they could fuck, he placed the barrel of his revolver to her soft pink lips.

"Pretend that this a big black dick, like the one you just finished sucking on." Slowly he stood up with the gorilla in her face as he fixed his pants. "Where Teck and Wallo?" he asked.

"Huh?"

"Bitch, you know the saying: If you can say huh, you can hear. Yeah, I know all about what you did to my sister!"

Constance slid back toward the headboard, shivering. "What are you talking about?" she screamed.

He tried to quiet her by smacking her upside the head with the gun. Just his luck, he did it too hard and opened a bleeding gash near her hairline. She was stunned.

"Where they at?" he hissed in her ear.

"S-storage," she cried, frightened by the blood trickling down her face.

"What?"

"S-storage. . . . He's gone to get his van in Clayton."

"Did the twins kill my sister?"

"Yes." She nodded. The blood was beginning to collect in the corner of her mouth.

"They shot my sister the first time too?" He yanked her hair back.

"Yes," she cried.

Anshon couldn't help the tears falling from his eyes. "Bitch, you could've told me about the twins. Then my sister would be alive!" Anshon pulled the trigger back and shot Constance twice in the head as she spent her last breath begging for her life. "And that's on the strength of you, Tammy," Anshon mumbled. He spit on Constance's body on his way out. "Dumb bitch!"

Teck was halfway to Clayton when he realized he'd left the keys to the storage unit in Constance's bedroom. He made a quick U-turn then gunned the engine, bringing the front wheel in the air. When the wheel touched the pavement, he was going 91 miles per hour. He reached Redwood in record-breaking time.

He left his helmet on as he went up to the door and knocked. When she didn't answer, he opened the door with his brother's key. Once inside, he called out her name as he slid the tinted visor up. He ran up the stairs and called her name once again.

He opened the bedroom door. "Yo, Constance, I forgot—" He paused at the sight before him. "Constance!" he shouted "What the fuck! Constance!"

Constance's blood was flowing from the bed and covered half the floor. Teck pulled off his helmet and fell to his knees. "What the fuck happened?" he shouted.

He jumped up and raced out the door. Not knowing where he would end up, he knew he had to get the hell out. He hopped on his bike, and before he realized where he was headed, he found himself pulling up to Fe-Fe's.

Fe-Fe was still curled up in the bed when her doorbell rang. She jumped up and ran toward the door, praying it was Anshon. She looked at the person standing at her door and saw it was the real Teck.

"Oh my God!" she screamed. "Wallo tried to rape me." She fell into Teck's arms. "Teck, can you believe it? He's upstairs!"

Teck pushed her away and started calling for his brother to come downstairs. "Wallo! Wallo!"

Wallo jumped up and ran down the stairs.

"I know what the plan was," Teck said, "but somebody else killed Constance. It's some shit in the game."

"What!" Wallo screamed.

Teck took a deep breath then explained to his brother how he had found Constance. Teck and Wallo were so upset about not knowing what the hell was going on that they didn't pay Fe-Fe any mind as she went to her bedroom. She called Anshon on his cell phone.

She quickly told Anshon that the twins were over and that some crazy shit was going down. Just as she was about to mention Constance, she heard the phone click off.

Fe-Fe quickly got dressed and quietly ran back down the stairs. She tipped into the kitchen and grabbed a knife. She wanted to sneak out the back door, but she was scared the twins might hear her and shoot her, so she just laid low with a knife tucked under the hoodie she had on.

In the living room, she found Wallo sitting on the couch with his face buried in his hands, crying as Teck paced the floor with his cell phone to his ear, trying to call Kristi.

Teck was shook. He couldn't reach Kristi. He pushed the REDIAL button for the third time.

"Baby, please pick up," he said as he tapped his fist to his lips. After the ninth ring, he hung up. "I'm out. Stay here until I get back," Teck instructed. "I'ma go see Kristi."

"Fe-Fe," Teck said, looking around the room, "don't let him leave. And Wallo, don't fuck with her." Teck headed for the door.

"Nigga, dis ain't Holiday fuckin' Inn!" she snapped. "Both y'all asses can step!" She pointed toward the front door.

Teck turned around and pointed the black .40 cal at Fe-Fe's chest. "You heard what the fuck I said! Now talk slick and see if I don't make light shine through your body!"

Fe-Fe wasn't stupid. She nodded her head up and down.

When Teck stepped outside, Selma's finest were slowly riding down the street three deep. They saved his life, because Anshon, Wood C, and Deck were sitting in the cut, waiting on his ass.

Anshon looked at his boys. "He got away for now and only now."

Fe-Fe sat on her couch with her arms folded as Wallo sat at the other end, crying. When two taps sounded at the door, it flew open before Fe-Fe could answer it. Anshon came in, followed by Wood C and Deck. Wallo figured he was still in the clear. He didn't look up until he heard Fe-Fe say, "Oh, shit!"

He looked up to see Anshon standing over him with the biggest revolver he'd ever seen in his life. Fe-Fe stood up, but Wood C motioned for her to sit down.

"Why, muthafucka?" Anshon sobbed. "What the fuck my sister ever do wrong to your bitch ass?"

Wallo lowered his head.

"Answer me!" Anshon shouted, placing the barrel on Wallo's forehead.

Wallo shrugged his shoulders then placed his hand on the armrest of the couch. Fe-Fe started to scream.

Anshon looked at her.

"He got a .380 stashed between the seats," she said.

Before Anshon could do anything, Deck punched Wallo in the mouth then picked up the .380. Wood C was at the window with his two heaters.

Anshon glanced at Fe-Fe as tears filled her eyes. He didn't have to speak. He nodded his head once.

"Where Teck go?" Anshon asked Wallo.

Wallo's mouth was bleeding badly. He wiped his mouth, shrugging his shoulders.

"Nigga, he just left!" Anshon said then hit him with the .50 upside his head before he told another lie.

"Fuck you. Ain't givin' up my brother," Teck said.

"My sister dead 'cause of your ass!" Anshon screamed. After that was said, he handed his revolver to Deck then started to pound Wallo with hard blows to the face and body.

Fe-Fe wanted to feel sorry for Wallo, but she couldn't. After all, he had tried to rape her and he killed Tammy.

When Deck told Anshon to ease up, Wallo was left on the floor with his face badly bruised up. Fe-Fe started to cry as Anshon took her to the back room after she told them where Teck was headed. When he closed Fe-Fe's bedroom door behind him, she broke down and asked him not to kill her.

"What?" he asked her, surprised. "I love you. I'm in love with you. Why would I kill you?"

Fe-Fe didn't know what to say, so she fell into his arms.

"I know we can't be together, so I've been trying to fight this shit, but it gets harder every day."

Fe-Fe's mouth dropped open. "Anshon . . . I—I'm pregnant."

"Damn, baby." Anshon rubbed her face.

"Don't worry now," she assured him. "Please don't."

"Okay, okay," he said, trying to shake what Fe-Fe had just told him.

"The twins killed Tammy, Fe-Fe. You know I gotta do what I gotta do."

Fe-Fe hugged him. "I'm on your side, Anshon. Always know that." She stood on her toes and kissed him on the forehead before he left. She caught him by his shirt as he was turning to leave. "I love you."

He winked his eye at her and ran back down the stairs. Fe-Fe prayed that she would see him again.

Teck made it back to Selma two hours later. Because he was in a panic and speeding, he'd led five highway state patrols on a high-speed chase, until he lost them on a back road in Wilson Mills. He didn't care, because he was still in shock after finding Kristi's body at her duplex.

Kristi wasn't supposed to die. That was the deal he and Wallo had. It was supposed to only be Constance.

What the fuck is going on? Teck thought.

Teck felt pain and hate at the same time. He pulled up in Fe-Fe's driveway and found a note on the front door. He instantly recognized his brother's handwriting and didn't try to reason why his brother wanted him to go to the school bus parking lot at Triple S. He took the back roads and hit Buffalo Road.

When he reached the parking lot, he spotted his brother's forest green Nissan Quest parked in front of the gym with its lights off. When he neared the Nissan Quest, he noticed the driver's side window was down, and with a closer inspection, he saw his brother slumped over the wheel.

He brought his motorcycle to a screeching halt and jumped off. Teck was reaching for the Quest's door handle when suddenly the side door slid back.

"Yeah, nigga!" Deck said, pointing the MAC-11 at Teck's chest.

When Teck looked at who he thought was his brother, he saw Wood C grinning at him, gold fronts and all. "See you in hell, pot'nah!"

Teck turned slowly to see Anshon stepping from behind the minivan, holding the golden .50-cal pointed at his head. Teck wasn't as brave as his brother. He threw his hands up in defeat.

Wood C stepped out and relieved Teck of his .40. Teck had never felt so much fear in his life as Wood C yanked his helmet off.

"Look at me!"Anshon shouted.

Teck slowly turned his head toward Anshon as the gold barrel touched his forehead.

"You was my ma'fuckin' pot'nah, nigga. We stole on niggas together, and this is the shit that you do?" Anshon spat on him. "I remember when I came home from prison, I told you that if I caught the muthafuckers that fucked wit' my sis—" Anshon's hand was trembling. Flashes of Tammy's casket being lowered into the ground kept playing in his mind. Then he thought of his niece and nephew growing up without her.

"Motherfucker!" Before pulling the trigger, he wanted to ask Teck why, but deep down he didn't want to know.

Wood C took a step back as Anshon wiped his eyes. Deck did the same. Wood C happened to glance toward the road to see two sets of headlights coming. "Yo, Shon, wait."

BOOM! Too late.

As the state troopers' cars drove nearer, they heard the echoing sound from the blast, and the flash from the barrel was bright and distinctive. Instantly, the lead state trooper hit the blue lights and the gas.

Wood C took off running toward the lunchroom. Deck stepped in front of the minivan and made the MAC-11 speak. Anshon ran toward the gym and fired a shot at the lock. Deck was on his heels two seconds later. They could hear the two state troopers sliding to a halt as they busted through the double doors, looking for their suspects.

Wood C had crept his way to the student parking lot and was still moving. He headed for the woods to hopefully disappear before the backup K-9 unit came. Wood C loved his freedom. Fuck prison.

Anshon and Deck were just running past the front office when the two state troopers let off with their glock 9 mm. Deck slid to the floor and rolled to his right, as Anshon dove to the left. They could both hear the state troopers calling for backup.

Deck stuck the MAC-11 around the corner and squeezed off eight shots. The barrage sent the state troopers for cover. Deck got up and took off running while changing the empty 32-round clip.

As Deck ran for the lunchroom, Anshon made his move. It was hard to fire on the run with the .50. Its kickback was too big for a one-hand shot. He was breathing heavily as he took off toward the library. It was better to split up. He knew he would never see the free world if he was caught. He quickly reloaded the two empty shots in his .50 with shaky hands.

"Fuck!" he whispered at the sounds of police sirens in the distance. He lowered himself to his stomach and moved quickly behind a row of books in the pitch black library. When he heard the chatter of the police radio near the door, he stopped breathing in hopes they hadn't seen him enter the library. Niggas get a sixth sense when they're on the run.

"Police!" a deep, commanding voice shouted. "Come out with your hands up!"

Anshon closed his eyes and murmured a quick prayer, but why would God listen to a sinner? He was the bad guy.

"Last warning!" the state trooper stated.

Anshon gripped the gold .50 and kissed the barrel. He had made up his mind to save one round. He refused to live and die in prison.

"You and me, baby girl," he whispered, hyping himself up. He slowly came up on one knee and peeked between some books. He only saw one of the state troopers as he ducked behind the checkout counter, gun in hand.

His heart was pounding in his ears. He searched for the second state trooper but came up short. He slowly slid a thick hardcover book from the shelf. The police sirens were still in the distance. He had to get ghost before the backup showed up. He gripped the book, slung it clear across the library, and was moving in the opposite direction before it struck the computer room door.

The hidden state trooper made his presence known by squeezing off two loud shots in the area where he saw the book thrown from.

Anshon dove to the floor. These mutha-fuckas wasn't playing anymore. He cocked back the hammer and turned just in time to catch the state trooper in the moonlight as he moved from behind the checkout counter.

Anshon brought up the gorilla with a firm two-hand grip while on one knee. He knew he had to go all out. He eased back on the trigger. *BOOM!* Then he rolled to his left.

The hidden state trooper, who was calling his partner over, saw how the impact of the gun lifted him off his feet completely, and he flipped back over the checkout counter. The .50 packed so much power that it took the state trooper's entire right arm off.

Anshon heard the hidden state trooper gasp in shock near the reading lounge.

BOOM! BOOM! BOOM! Glass shattered from the buzzing slugs from the .50. He took off for the door while he had the chance. Just as he exited the library, the police backup slid into the student dropoff loop, six deep. He took off toward the lunchroom.

"Officer down!" he heard someone scream behind him. "Down the hall, freeze!"

By instinct, he dove to the glossy floor, sliding on his stomach as the deadly line of lead ripped down the hall. They kept firing down the dark hallway, trying to pin Anshon down. Anshon could see blue lights out in the student parking lot. They were trying to trap him off.

They were still firing as he rolled toward the hallway leading to the brick masonry class. Once in the hallway, he stumbled to his feet and took off running full speed. He had to hit the back exit and try to get ghost in the woods. He was on pure adrenalin as he reached the fire exit.

The alarm blared once he burst through the fire exit. A sheriff's deputy patrol car was slowing to a stop just as his feet touched the pavement.

BOOM! The entire front windshield exploded. The rookie deputy was leaning over and looked up where the headrest used to be. He shifted in reverse without ever looking up. He planned to resign tomorrow.

Anshon ran between two outside trailer-like classrooms and quickly reloaded the five empty slots. Taking four quick breaths, he dashed across the band practice field and headed for the woods. The police were done with a verbal warning. The trooper that Anshon had shot in the library was dead.

Anshon had reached the woods, then he tripped over a log. When he struggled to his feet, he turned to see countless moving flashlights, and in the center was the barking K-9. He turned and bent down over the long barrel. He didn't know if his shot would reach, but he'd let 'em know what would be waiting.

Back at the fire exit, the K-9 officer was about to let his dog go, when suddenly a deputy standing five feet from him holding a pump was thrown back on his ass, followed by the report from Anshon's .50.

BOOM! They all scattered. They couldn't return any fire because there were houses not far from the woods. The slug had reached out and touched the deputy in the upper chest. It didn't punch through the vest, but the slug packed enough stopping power to make the deputy's heart stop.

Anshon was already on the run when the deputy hit the ground. He ran a good distance, until he found the running trail used by the track and field team. He stopped and crouched to the ground. He could see them searching the woods to his left.

He placed the .50 on the ground and quickly took his Nikes off. He removed both socks then found two rocks. He had to trick that fucking K-9 if he wanted to stand any chance of getting away. He wiped both socks under his arms and vigorously wiped his ass with them. He then placed a rock in each sock and quickly pissed on both.

The time to complete his deception took forty-eight seconds. He slung one to the left and then slung the other to the right, then took off running with the gold .50 at a measured pace. He'd run for thirty to forty seconds, then stop and listen. He repeated this until he circled out of the woods near the football practice field. He could see countless squad cars in the bus parking lot.

Teck's minivan was parked in the same spot, and when a police car pulled off, he saw the lights shining on the nearly headless Teck, who'd been killed and pushed under his minivan earlier.

Anshon watched and caught his breath. Just because it was dark, he knew it didn't mean he was safe or well hidden. Two minutes later, he made his move to cross the road. Once he made it safely across the street, he ran through the field. Once he reached the woods, he knew he'd be straight.

He reached the thick woods and ran through a briar patch. The thorns hooked him in a thousand spots, but it would take more than some thorns to stop him from running from the police. Since he still had on the gloves, he pulled the briars loose and surged deeper into the woods.

When he reached a cow field, he slowed up. He took the time to catch his breath once again and loaded the one empty chamber, leaving him with four slugs in his pocket and five in the golden chamber. He nearly shitted on himself when his cell phone rang.

"Shit!" He lowered himself closer to the ground and silenced the ringer.

"Yeah, who dis?" he said, licking his dry lips.

"Wood C, nigga. Where you at?" Wood C whispered.

"Near a cow field," Anshon replied then shot the same question back to Wood C.

"Hiding in somebody's back yard under a truck," Wood C whispered. "Deck ain't answering his phone. You seen 'im?"

"We split up at the school," Anshon whispered while looking around with quick jerks.

"Yo . . . I'ma holla."

"A'ight."

When he slid the slim phone back into his chest pocket, he went back on the move. The cows ignored him as he crouched down near the fence. He thought of his sister as he stood up to jog across another field.

The pain was still there. His quest for revenge hadn't changed a damn thing, except his fate. Tammy's words of advice rang in his mind: *Don't let the game be your demise.*

Anshon prayed to God to let him reach Peedin Street. If not, he'd be beggin' for the Lord to let him in Heaven's door. So he kept running.

He knew he had to be careful crossing Highway 70, so he paused at the edge of the woods and waited for the right chance. Anshon realized the spot he was in was spelling out his life to him. He could see the overpass, and further down 70 to his left was a place he never wanted to see again: prison. To his right and a few miles down the road was the cemetery, a place where his sister and Momma rested in peace, a place he wasn't ready to visit just yet, but if it came down to it, he'd pick the right over the left. That left nothing but moving forward to reach home.

He said Monica's name, laced up his kicks, cocked the hammer back, and dashed across the four-lane highway. His inspection didn't pick out the two Selma's finest parked in the cut.

"Freeze! Police!"

Chapter 11

Monica sat at her kitchen table next to Fe-Fe, with her hand on her cell phone and the cordless on the table. The two women were both worried about the same man. When Fe-Fe told Monica about the twins, she nearly fainted. There was no doubt in her mind that Anshon would kill them both. She just wanted her man to come home. Fuck everything else.

"You sure they didn't tell you where they took Wallo?" Monica asked with tears running down her face.

Fe-Fe shook her head slowly side to side. They both had their car keys within reach, and when Monica's cordless phone rang, she answered it before the first ring was completed.

"Hello!"

She prayed she would hear Anshon's voice. It was Deck. He told her that he needed a ride and that he would meet her at the Pizza Hut in Smithfield. Deck had put some miles on his Reeboks and was in the clear. He had ditched his MAC-11. When he told her that Wood C and Anshon was still on the run, she nearly dropped the phone.

Fe-Fe rushed to pick it up, and Deck repeated everything he'd just said to Monica. Fe-Fe snatched up her keys and ran out the door to go pick up the stranded Deck. Monica sat back down and started to cry uncontrollably. She wanted Anshon.

Wood C had somehow made it to McDonald's on 301 and was now sitting in the front eating his meal and trying to blend in. Police were still heading down toward the high school. He'd broke his cell phone when he dove from a pair of headlights as he crept through the white neighborhood next to the school's campus. Once he was in the clear, he dropped his two .40s in a plastic trashcan. He planned to calm his nerves down then bum a ride back to Selma, which he guessed would be easy.

He was biting into his Quarter Pounder when he saw Fe-Fe's Legend slow down for a red light on 301.

Fe-Fe was still praying for Anshon as she sat at the red light. It was a long wait, and just as she came off the brake, Wood C swung the door open, scaring the shit out of Fe-Fe.

"Go, go, go, go, go, go, go, go, go, go!" Wood C said, slamming the door. She pulled off.

They both tried to talk at the same time. Fe-Fe won. She told him about Deck then asked about

Anshon. Wood C was happy to hear about Deck, but as of now, Anshon was still on the run.

"Once we pick up Deck, hit Buffalo Road. Lemme see your cell phone." He checked the side mirror—no blue lights.

Fe-Fe told him she didn't have a cell phone.

"Damn!" he said, slamming his fist on the dashboard.

Deck was standing in the parking lot when they pulled up. When he saw Wood C, he asked about Anshon as he got into the back seat. Deck pulled out his phone and quickly dialed Anshon's cell number. He didn't answer.

"Roadblock." Fe-Fe sighed as they rounded the corner near Smithfield Middle School. Blue lights were everywhere.

"Fuck!" Wood C said.

When a helicopter flew over with a blinding spotlight, Wood C clenched his fists. The police had Buffalo Road locked down and made them turn around.

Anshon was on the run again, and this time they were on his ass. He had followed their command to freeze, but a passing eighteen-wheeler had blinded the four police that were two deep in each squad car.

Anshon made the .50 throw up. He eased back on the trigger, making the gorilla erupt in his hand. *Boom!* A slug punched a police in the chest, killing him instantly. *Boom!* A slug flattened a tire. *Boom!* A slug shattered the second squad car's side window.

He took off for the woods and reloaded the .50 on the run. Five shots left. God had to be looking down on him when he tripped over a tree stump, as the police opened up with an AR-15, talking in rapid succession. Branches fell on his back as the rapid fire continued to blaze over his head.

He fired one shot over his shoulders. *Boom!*

When the helicopter roared over the treetops with its bright light, he became disoriented. He got himself together, came to his feet, and ran. Fuck looking back; he wanted to move forward. Thorns cut into his face and neck, tearing at his skin, but he kept moving without missing a step. Pain would come later. His chest was on fire, but he kept running.

When he ran into the dog pound, he knew he was almost home. He was about to cut to the right when something hot hit him in the arm, spinning him around. He slammed into a tree. He rolled over to his stomach and easily found the gleaming .50.

His left arm had been hit by a stray round. Ignoring his useless arm, he got up and ran. He could hear the police yelling out to each other as the helicopter buzzed the treetops with its blinding light.

He dove to the ground just as the spotlight moved over him. He gritted his teeth and willed his wounded arm to support the .50. He raised it up as the spotlight moved near him. When the light blinded him, he eased back on the trigger.

BOOM! He completely missed the light, but the slang easily punched through the bottom-viewing window in the cockpit and hit the co-pilot in the stomach after the slug first traveled up through his leg.

The pilot shrieked and banked the helicopter in a tight turn as the co-pilot spewed blood all over the cockpit.

Taking a deep breath, Anshon got up and ran through the woods. He burst out of the woods, running as fast as he could. His heart was pounding, and sweat covered his face, which set his face on fire from the open cuts.

He ran in the angle that would allow him to go through his back yard. He could see Selma's finest accelerating down Peedin Street five deep with the blue lights flashing. Suddenly, Anshon stumbled and fell flat on his face.

Monica ran to the front door when the police rode by. Deck had called to tell her that Anshon was still on the run. Tears ran down her face as she looked down the road. Plum and Dee were also standing outside. "Baby, please." Monica cried to herself. "Please come home."

***

Deck was on his way back to Peedin Street with Fe-Fe. Wood C was now sitting behind a bush at the corner of Preston and Massey Street when he saw the K-9 unit coming. Just as it reached his hiding spot, he ran to the curb and emptied Deck's little .32.

POP, POP, POP, POP, POP, POP! It caused the driver to lose control and hit the curb at forty miles per hour, breaking the rim as the tire blew. Wood C hoped it would help. He took off running and vanished with ease.

Anshon was almost home, but he was past exhausted. He was now in the field behind his trailer. His cell phone didn't work, so he had to make a quiet entrance. He was bleeding badly, but the wound could have been worse. He fell to his knees then rolled to his side. He was too tired, too weak. He silently cried.

He got up once more but collapsed after five steps. As he was getting to his feet, he heard the K-9 and knew it would follow his blood trail, and if the dog didn't kill him, the police would.

He refused to go back to prison. "Big sis!" he sobbed as he held the .50 to his head. He closed his eyes and slowly eased back on the trigger. . . .

EPILOGUE

Ten Months Later
Selma, NC

Fe-Fe stood at the gravesite holding her two-month-old baby girl, Tammy, with grief resting in her heart. Next to her stood Monica, holding her six-week-old baby boy, Anshon, and she too had grief resting in her heart. They were both paying their respects to someone they cared about deeply and missed.

Monica placed a single red rose on the gravesite as tears rolled down her cheek. After they said their silent good-byes, they both turned to hug each other.

"You be safe, okay?" Fe-Fe said.

Monica wiped her eyes. "I will, Fe-Fe. Just stay in touch with me."

"I promise," Fe-Fe said before she turned to leave.

Monica watched her best friend slowly walk away. She was happy for Fe-Fe and Wood C, who were now together. Fe-Fe had legal custody

of her twins again, and the five of them lived up
in Richmond, Virginia. . . . Really it was six if
you wanted to count the new seed Wood C had
baking in Fe-Fe's oven.

Fe-Fe hated lying to Monica about Wood C
being li'l Tammy's father, but little did Fe-Fe
know, Monica knew the truth. The baby looked
too much like Anshon for anything to be denied.

As Wood C neared his gleaming 300C, he
opened the door for his queen then kissed her
lightly on the lips. They both waved good-bye
then slowly pulled out of the quiet cemetery, and
that was Fe-Fe's and Wood C's ending.

As for Deck, he was still in Selma. He now
ran a barbershop on Raiford that supported his
brand new triple-wide trailer out in Southern
Estates. He no longer took up space in Wood
C's 300C passenger seat. He now had Anshon's
Chevy.

Larrisha and her brother Von moved to Los
Angeles.

Monica neared the shiny QX56 then wiped
her teary eyes. She leaned over to kiss her baby.
A few moments later, they were heading for
I-95 South to begin a new life down in Miami,
Florida. Tammy had made her promise her
before she died that they would take the spot in
Miami as soon as Anshon got out of the game.

"Well, baby," Monica said, looking up to the
sky, "I guess this is it."

Enjoy this sample from:

Hold U Down
by Keisha Ervin

Available September 2016 in Mass Market paperback

1

Simply Unique

"I got no time for fake niggas . . . Just sip some Cristal with these real niggas . . . From East to West Coast we spread love niggas . . . And while you niggas talk shit we count bank figures," Unique sang with her eyes behind shades, strolling down the streets of L.A.

Fresh to death with Moschino bags, Unique and Tha Get Money Crew strutted down Robertson Boulevard, looking as if they could have been young socialites or *Sex and the City* knockoffs. Unique, a.k.a. Nique, Kiara, Kay Kay, and Zoë had the best of everything—great looks, cars with chrome spinners, designer outfits, and money.

None of them needed a man for anything, but most of the niggas they fucked wit' were tricks. It was nothing for a man to pay all of their bills. The girls always stayed fly. They all lived life by their own rules. Falling in love was a no-no. To them, men were looked upon as pawns, mere playthings. Catching feelings was forbidden and looked at as a sign of disloyalty. Only rough sex and getting money was allowed. Their motto, *Niggas Ain't Nothing but Hoes and Tricks,* was tattooed on each of their lower backs.

Kiara, a single mother of one, was the loud-mouth of the crew. Tall and caramel, with full lips and an attitude to match, Kiara butted heads with Unique often. Kay Kay, her identical twin, was the peacemaker, silent type. She kept it gully and always kept her feelings close to her heart. Zoë, the feisty, petite, mahogany-colored mamacita held it down for real. She was down for whatever, even if it meant putting her own life in danger.

Unique, the leader of the clique, had one thing and one thing only on her mind at all times—money. It kept her alive and on the grind, thirsting for more. Hustling was the song she sang, and getting money was all she knew. The only men she ever loved were dead ones—Benjamin Franklin and Andrew Jackson.

With smooth peanut butter skin, big brown eyes, Egyptian cheekbones, plump lips, red hair with blonde highlights, and a pretty smile to match, she captured the male species' hearts. Reaching about five foot five in height, Unique wasn't a slim chick. Her hips rounded out to be size ten, and her full breasts filled out a C cup bra. On her left shoulder she had a set of praying hands tattooed with the words *Lord Forgive Me* underneath. To most, she was considered a lethal weapon. She was often compared to the singer Keyshia Cole, but to her crew, she was just their girl and the one who called all the shots.

"Niggas ain't shiiiit!" Unique stomped her foot, slamming her Nextel shut.

"What did Tone do now?" Kiara asked.

"That was Patience. She told me she saw Tone riding down Lucas and Hunt with Robin! Then she said that her friend Chantell's sister seen him at Toxic later on that night Big Willyin' it up."

"Ain't she the same chick that blew his cell phone up last week?" Zoë questioned.

"Yeah, that's her. I swear to God I hate that black muthafucka. He thinks just because he pays all of my bills that he can cheat and do whatever he wants."

"I don't know why men think they can cheat, like we won't find out." Zoë shook her head and laughed.

"Because they stupid, that's why! They think with their penises and not their brains, stupid bastards!"

"Just hit them pockets up when you get home."

"That's what's up, but have you seen that bitch? She ugly than a muthafucka," Kay Kay added.

"The bitch is wack! She's a broke, bummy, Reebok broad! I mean, come on, look at me! How the fuck he gon' cheat on me with a project chick?" Unique stated, looking over her physique.

"Okay, bitch, you can quit feeling yourself, 'cause remember pussy don't have no face." Zoë grinned.

"I don't know why you getting mad. It ain't like you gon' leave him." Kiara rolled her eyes and sucked her teeth.

"That's not the point! It's the principle of the whole thing! As long as that nigga continue to provide for me then I'm good to go! But it pisses me off because the nigga be trying to act like it's all about me when he's out fuckin' other hoes! But you know what? It's all good because I'm getting mine in the end. Love should never be in the equation when it comes to a relationship anyway, 'cause once you allow yourself to love that muthafucka, everything in your life becomes about him and eventually you lose yourself!" Staring off into space, Unique knew that her speech was more about her mother than herself.

"Look, when it all boils down to it, you getting paid, so fuck all that other bullshit and continue to get money," Zoë assured.

"Right, so calm down. You should be used to the shit by now. Y'all been fuckin' around forever, and he has cheated the whole time. Ain't none of this shit new to you," Kiara continued.

"Yeah, just keep on tagging them pockets every time he fuck up," Kay Kay chimed in.

"Fuck all this bullshit. We gotta hurry and get back to the hotel so we can do this shit," Unique said, shaking off the whole situation.

"So, what's the deal wit' your boy, Nique?" Kiara asked.

"I set it up for him to meet me at The Ivy at eight o'clock. Eric's gonna have this valet guy named Thomas to park the Murcielago around the back in the far right corner of the parking lot."

"So, basically all I have to do is get the keys from Eric."

"Yeah, but I told him that you would give him the other three hundred when you got the keys."

"Shit, this crackin' up to be one of our easiest licks ever." Zoë grinned.

"Don't get it twisted. You never know what could happen," Unique cautioned as she eyed a green Foley dress in the Lisa Kline store window.

"Yo, chill, Nique. Don't nobody want to hear that shit before a lick," Kiara said, annoyed.

"This real talk. If you don't like it then don't listen. Y'all hoes need to realize that we could get knocked at any moment for this shit. Don't let this money go to yo' head." Unique checked her as the wind blew through her hair.

"Yeah, I am feeling myself too much, ain't I?"

"As usual."

"Yo, Nique, I just got a text from that nigga Bub up in VA," Zoë declared, going through her two-way.

"Hit that nigga back and see what's up," Unique replied, still entranced by the dress.

"Yeah, that nigga had a bad-ass Mercedes-Benz." Kay Kay nodded her head.

"Right. We can make at least a fifty Gs off that," Kiara added.

"I know, right? Let me hit this nigga up right now," Zoë said, getting excited.

After hitting a couple more stores, Unique and the girls headed back to the hotel to prepare for the heist. Looking at her reflection in the mirror, Unique wondered just how long she could continue stealing cars for a living. She and her cousins had been in the game for three years, but recently the life had begun to take a toll on her soul. Unique's pockets stayed on swole, but her conscience was eating her up every day.

She constantly wondered if old victims were out to get her. The shit had her paranoid. Something inside told her that something was about to jump off, but she just couldn't pinpoint it. Money kept on coming in, and her clientele continued to grow, but being the leader of a banging organization didn't satisfy her anymore. Yeah, Unique had the fringe benefits of clothes, jewelry, and cars, but Cezar, the guy she worked for, was the one who really saw the most dough. He was the real balla.

Two years after meeting Tone, her boyfriend of five years, Unique had linked up with Cezar. He was a good-looking, get-money nigga from the south side of St. Louis. Even though he was fine, Unique didn't look at him like that. She saw something more in Cezar than just being his girl-friend or chick on the side. Unique needed a side hustle, and Cezar was the perfect nigga to help her get on the grind. Refusing to hit the block, Unique decided to do what she did best—steal.

After a little research, she learned that Cezar already had a small ring of car thieves on his payroll. The little crew of niggas he had working for him wasn't really pulling in dough, so Unique, being the chick she was, offered her services. At first, Cezar was a little apprehensive because to him, a chick wouldn't know anything about steal-ing cars. Underestimating her talents because of her gender, Cezar slept on Unique's skills.

After recruiting her cousins to be a part of her crew, Unique hit the ground running. As a test, Cezar gave her and the girls the task of stealing an '03 Cadillac STS worth sixty grand. He just knew that Unique would be calling him from jail, begging him to bail her out; but he was wrong. Unique and the girls not only copped the STS, but for show they copped a Mercedes-Benz as well. Cezar was dumfounded to say the least. In a matter of months, Unique and Tha Get Money Crew stole over a half million dollars' worth of cars.

Stepping out of the bathroom, she asked, "How do I look?"

"You look fly as hell, ma," Zoë replied.

"Yeah, even with that ugly-ass wig you got on, you look good," Kiara joked.

"Fuck you." Unique smirked, putting her middle finger up.

"That dress is bad. You gon' have to let me borrow that when we go out."

"That's cool, but look, I'm running late, so give me a hug." Standing in a circle, they all wrapped their arms around one another and hugged. "Y'all know that we gotta be safe and discreet. I love you, and I'll meet you at the airport."

"A'ight, we love you too," Kay Kay replied.

"A'ight then, I'm up," Unique said as she left out the door with her bags in tow.

Pulling up to The Ivy, Unique searched for Rico's car, but she didn't spot him. She then looked for Eric. He was right in place. After she smoothed her dress down, she stepped out of her rented Lexus SC 430 and handed him the keys. Unique turned her attention to the busy intersection as she heard a loud engine soaring up the street.

Spotting Rico, she smiled. His yellow Lamborghini stood out among the sea of conservative vehicles. Waving at him, she caught his attention. As he got out, Unique couldn't help but be attracted to him. Tall, handsome, and muscular were the only words to describe him.

"You take this one. I'm tired," Eric said to Thomas, baiting him.

"You look beautiful." Rico kissed Unique's left cheek.

"Thank you. You look nice as well."

"Can I take your keys, sir?" Thomas, the anxious valet driver, asked.

"I'm not sure if I want to do the valet thing tonight."

"I promise that your car will be returned to you in tip-top shape, sir. I'm the best valet driver here," Thomas boasted. Looking at him, Unique saw that Eric was right—Thomas was a suck-up.

"Sweetie, this is a very nice restaurant. Your car will be safe," Unique added as she put her hand on his shoulder for reassurance.

"I don't think you understand, Lisa. This is a Murcielago. This car is worth ten of their yearly salaries," Rico said, calling Unique by one of her many aliases and not even knowing it. Wanting to smack the holy shit out of him for being so rude but holding her tongue, Unique tried to reason with him.

"Baby, trust me. Everything will be fine," she spoke seductively into his ear.

"I don't know, Lisa. I'd rather park it myself," he said, confused and turned on at the same time.

"If you let them park the car for you, I promise I will give you a very special treat tonight," Unique purred, massaging his dick.

"Um, sir, have you made up your mind? We have other people waiting," Thomas asked, eying Unique's hand moving in a circular motion.

"All right, but make sure you keep a close eye on my baby," Rico instructed, throwing Thomas the keys.

"Yes, sir. I will."

Forty-five minutes later, Unique and Rico sat gazing into each other's eyes as they ate lobster and steak. Slow, tranquil music played in the background as Rico became lost in her eyes while he thought about the promise she had made to him earlier. Already bored, Unique stared off into space, ignoring his every word.

"Lisa, did you hear me? I said dessert just arrived."

"I'm sorry, baby. My mind was somewhere else." Checking her watch, Unique excused herself from the table and went into the restroom. Pulling out her cell, she called Zoë.

"Y'all there yet?" she asked.

"Yeah, we just pulled up."

"A'ight."

"A'ight then, one," Zoë said, hanging up.

Flipping her phone closed, Unique took one last look in the mirror and walked back into the restaurant. Rico smiled when he saw her walking toward him. Once she got near the table, he got up and pulled her seat out for her, wanting to be a gentleman.

"How about after dinner we head over to this nice little jazz club that I know about around the corner?" Rico suggested.

"That sounds nice," Unique said, giving her best fake smile. Sensing that he was a little on edge, she asked, "What's wrong?"

"You know, I'm kinda worried about leaving my keys with the valet. There have been a lot of auto thefts in this area the last couple of months."

"Rico, stop worrying about that car and let's just enjoy the evening," she said, rubbing his hand and trying to ease his worries.

"Nah, I think I need to go out and check on my baby." He eased up out of his chair.

"No!" Unique blurted louder than she should have. Giving her a suspicious look, Rico stopped dead in his tracks.

"I'm sorry for yelling. It's just that I came to enjoy myself, not babysit your car. The car is insured, right?"

"Yeah."

"Okay then, there's no reason to worry," she assured, walking behind him and pushing his seat back up to the table so that he wouldn't go anywhere.

Sitting back down, Unique took his hand, gazed into his eyes, and whispered, "I promise, if you be a good little boy, you'll have a night that you will never forget." She smiled as she played footsies with his dick under the table.

"Girl, you gon' be the death of me." He smiled back gullibly.

"You just don't know," she whispered underneath her breath while checking her watch once more.

"You got the keys?" Kiara asked Eric in a low voice outside of the restaurant.

"Right here. You got my money?"

"Yeah, I got yo' money, nigga. Here," she said, placing three crisp, new hundred-dollar bills in his hand.

"You know that I could get fired for this."

"Nigga, quit whining and give me the keys so I can bounce," Kiara said, surveying her surroundings and making sure no one was looking.

Quietly passing the keys to her, Eric went back to work as usual. Dressed like she was out having a good time, Kiara headed around back to the parking area. Cool, calm, and collected, she played the role perfectly while putting on a pair of black gloves. Knowing that the restaurant didn't have any security cameras in the parking lot, she deactivated the alarm and got in without leaving a trace behind. The valet driver, Thomas, never even saw her pull off the lot.

Skipping dessert, Unique informed Rico that she was ready to leave so that they could get the festivities started.

"Baby, while you pay the check, I'm gonna go freshen up." She kissed his cheek.

"A'ight, baby. I'm gon' be outside waiting," Rico said while eyeing her ass.

Once in the bathroom, Unique dialed Kay Kay's cell phone number.

"It's here," Kay Kay replied without saying hello.

"A'ight. I'll meet you at LAX in about an hour."

"One," Kay Kay said, hanging up.

Checking her reflection in the mirror, Unique saw that her eyes were red. Going through her purse she found a tiny bottle of Visine. The blue contacts in her eyes were irritating the hell out of her. After dropping a few drops in each eye, she fingered through her black wig and touched up her makeup. The contacts and wig were all a part of her disguise. None of Unique's victims really knew how she looked.

Meeting Rico back outside, Unique saw him in a heated argument with the valet driver.

"I swear, sir, I don't know what happened," Thomas tried to explain.

"I trusted you with my car, man! Where the fuck is it?" Rico yelled.

"What's wrong, sweetie?" Unique asked, pretending to be concerned.

"My car is gone! I told you we couldn't trust these muthafuckas. You betta hope yo' shit is still here." Giving Eric her valet ticket, Unique listened to Rico's whining until her car pulled around the corner.

"My car is here," she replied.

"What am I gon' do without my baby?" Rico cried.

"I'm so sorry. This is all my fault. I shouldn't have suggested that you leave your car with them," Unique said, conjuring up some fake tears.

"Baby, don't cry. This is not your fault." Rico hugged her. "It's this idiot's fault," he said, pointing to Thomas. "Not yours."

"So, what do you want to do?" Unique questioned, dabbing tears from her eyes.

"I'm gonna stay here and fill out a police report. You go on back to the hotel. I'll call you later."

"Okay," she said, kissing and hugging him good-bye.

Securely in the rental car, Unique gave Rico another wave while thinking, *Good riddance, you stupid fuck.* Whipping the car out into the busy intersection, she never looked back.

A couple of blocks away, parked and relieved that the job was almost over, she pulled off the wig and exhaled a sigh of relief. Changing into a wife beater and jeans, she placed another wig on her head and drove to the rental place. Since everything was cool with the car, it only took her a total of fifteen minutes to drop it off.

After taking a shuttle bus to the airport, she checked her luggage in and headed for Gate 16. Once she reached the gate, she saw all three girls laughing and talking as if they hadn't just committed a crime.

"Y'all hoes sure do look cool, calm, and collected."

"What up, dawg?" Kay Kay smiled.

Taking a seat next to Zoë, Unique placed her carry-on luggage down beside her and began telling the story. "Girl, that nigga was so paranoid about leaving his car with the valet, it wasn't even funny."

"He was?"

"Yeah, I kept on having to reassure him that the damn car would be all right. He even kept calling it his *baby*."

"Damn, straight up? So, how did he react when he found out the car was stolen?" Kay Kay questioned.

"Girl, he went ballistic." Unique laughed.

"It's always funny to see the reaction on their faces. Where is he at now?"

"As far as I know he's still at the restaurant wondering where his car is. Oops, I mean, his *baby*."

"He's probably all like, 'Dude! Where's my car?'" Kay Kay laughed.

"Girl, you silly. Y'all FedExed the money to Patience, right?"

"Yeah, Nique, Zoë and I went before we came here."

"Y'all wrapped it up in newspaper and bubble wrap, right?"

"Yeah, they did. Damn, quit trippin'," Kiara said, annoyed. She slumped down in the seat with her arms folded across her chest.

"What the fuck is yo' problem?"

"Why is it every time we do a job you ask us the same stupid-ass questions over and over again? Ain't nobody gon' fuck up."

"Yo, who the fuck you think you talkin' to? Last time I checked, I ran this shit. Don't ever question me, 'cause I'm the one who has to answer to Cezar, not you."

"You still need to calm down. I get sick of you badgering us all the time."

"I badger you 'cause this shit will give us ten to life if we fuck up."

"Ten to life? You buggin'." Kiara waved her off, rolling her eyes.

"First of all, you need to shut the fuck up and play your position. I'm that bitch, and what I say goes. If you don't like it, step the fuck off. Kick rocks. The road is that way." Unique stood up, pointing her finger in Kiara's face.

"Yo, chill! We don't need this shit right now. We're cousins. Remember that," Kay Kay said, pulling Unique back.

Looking around at the other girls, Kiara tried to see if they agreed with her, but neither one of them said anything. To her, Zoë and Kay Kay were nothing but punks because they never stood up to Unique. Whatever she said, they went along with, but Kiara was sick of following Unique's rule.

"I'm sick of this. When we get home, give me my cut and don't say shit to me. I'm done fuckin' wit' you."

"Bye, bitch. You can take your money and step," Unique replied, heated.

"Everyone boarding Flight Sixteen from Los Angles to St. Louis please line up to board the plane," the flight attendant said over the loud-speaker. Grabbing her bag, Kiara pushed past the girls and got in line alone.

"She be on some dumb shit," Zoë said, shaking her head.

"Yeah, you better get yo' sister before I hurt her, Kay Kay," Unique added.

"I don't know what her problem is. She been trippin' lately," Kay Kay said, supporting Unique.

"All I know is she better come to me correct before I kill her ass," Unique snapped as they boarded the plane.

2

Got Me Trippin'

The weather in St. Louis was hot and muggy as Unique and the girls stood outside the airport awaiting their rides. Kiara and Unique were still not talking, and neither was willing to apologize. Catching each other's glances from time to time, they would roll their eyes at one another. The two had been bumping heads ever since they were little.

Unique didn't know if Kiara called herself being jealous or what the problem was. Either it was a snide remark coming out of her mouth, or she wanted to run the clique's business her way. Unique felt that if she could trust her with handling their affairs, she would, but Kiara was way too flashy and often ran her mouth too much to the wrong people. Kiara was too much of a loose cannon to run the business.

Any time they had beef, it was because of something Kiara said or did. As far back as she could remember, Unique always had to fight Kiara's battles, and frankly, she was getting tired of it.

As a matter of fact, she was getting tired of the whole thing. If they weren't cousins, she would have gotten rid of Kiara a long time ago.

Hugging Zoë good-bye, Unique watched as she climbed into her tender, Vito's '04 Chrysler 300C Hemi. Hailing down an airport cab, Unique hugged Kay Kay and told her that she would have her cut of the money by the following Monday. Not even acknowledging Kiara's presence, she jumped into the cab and headed home.

Riding past her old neighborhood on the north side of St. Louis, Unique asked the cab driver to make a quick detour. Pulling up, they parked in front of her old house on Beacon Avenue. Just seeing the house brought back so many memories for Unique—some good, some bad, some she wished had never happened, and some she wished she could experience again.

Unique reminisced about the times she spent with her mother, Syleena. Her mother was diagnosed with chronic schizophrenia when Unique was five. No matter how much medication she was given, she could never break loose of the brain disease. Unique tried to help her mother, but nothing she did seemed to make the situation better.

Syleena was in and out of mental clinics Unique's entire life. She saw her mother locked up and put in restraints too many times to remember. Unique and her little sister, Patience, were often sent to live with their Aunt Teresa, Kiara and Kay Kay's mom, when Syleena was sent away.

To make matters worse, Syleena blamed Unique for her mental state. As a teenager, Syleena was raped on her way home from school by an unidentified man and became pregnant. The police never caught him.

Being brought up in a heavily religious home, Syleena's parents refused to allow her to get an abortion. Syleena was distraught, to say the least. She hated the idea of having a rapist's baby. She tried everything to get rid of the fetus—everything from not eating to hitting herself in the stomach—but nothing worked.

By the time she was in her third trimester, Syleena came to the realization that no matter how much she wished and prayed the baby away, she was gonna have it. Still, she didn't like the idea. She detested the child inside of her. When Unique was born, she refused to hold or feed her. Syleena's mother had to do all the work. As Unique got older, the hatred her mother held toward her seemed to only manifest more. Syleena seriously thought that God was trying to punish her by having Unique, and she constantly reminded Unique of this. The words *You're a curse from God* replayed over and over in Unique's head.

Trying her best to make life easier for her mother, Unique began working at different fast food restaurants to support them, but the money wasn't enough. Bills were stacked up to the ceiling, the rent was past due, and every time she looked up she had a 42-year-old and a 12-year-old mouth to feed. Stealing was her only other option, so at the age of 18, Unique began helping herself to a five finger discount wherever she went, but that didn't work either. They were so far behind on the bills that one time when Syleena was sent away, Unique and Patience got evicted from their house.

With nowhere to go and only two hundred dollars saved up, Unique and Patience slept on the streets and ate fast food for meals. They could've gone over to their Aunt Teresa's house, but living on the streets was a far better choice. Teresa's house was like living in a death trap with a street name, but once Patience became sick, Unique saw that she had no other choice, and she took her sister to their aunt's house.

As they got off the bus, she saw that everything was still the same in the Walnut Park section of St. Louis: same old run-down houses, dirty-ass kids running around, crack fiends begging for a hit, and nickel-and-dime dealers on the streets. Shaking her head, Unique knew that she could only live this way for so much longer. She was tired of giving her all and still having nothing.

Walking three blocks, she found Aunt Teresa's house and knocked on the door.

"Who is it?"

"It's me," Unique mumbled, unsure of what to say.

"Me who, goddamnit!" her aunt yelled from the other side of the door.

"It's me, Unique, Aunt Teresa."

Cracking the door open, her aunt peeked her head through. "What you doing here? Ain't you supposed to be in a group home or something?"

"Nah, Auntie. Me and Patience were evicted from the house. Momma gone to the clinic again, and Patience is getting sick," she spoke, holding back the tears.

"Humph. Well, what you want from me?"

"I wanted to know if we could stay here for a little while, you know, until I get on my feet."

"You got some money? I know you got some ends."

"Yeah, but all I got is fifty dollars," Unique lied, rolling her eyes. Her aunt couldn't care less about them. At the end of the day, she was all about the bucks.

"Well, give it to me, and I want another two in a month, so you gon' have to get a job," she said, finally opening the door. "Kiara and Kay Kay, yo' cousins here!"

"What's up?" Kiara spoke, coming out of her room and looking Unique up and down.

"Hey, Nique. Hey Patience." Kay Kay greeted them both with a hug.

"Hi," Patience spoke softly.

"What's up?" Unique spoke too.

"Sista, I'm hungry." Patience tugged on her arm.

"Now look! Y'all ain't gon' be coming over here eating up all my goddamn food. And it's only two bedrooms in here, so y'all gon' have to sleep on the floor," Aunt Teresa yelled.

"No problem." *I've slept in worse places*, Unique thought. "I'll get you something to eat, Patience. Don't worry."

"It's getting late and I'm getting ready to go out, so make yourselves at home," Aunt Teresa said, grabbing her purse. With a fifty-dollar bill in hand, Harrah's Casino began to call her name.

Placing her bag on the floor, Unique sat down on the couch and surveyed the room. The once-white walls were now gray, the carpet was dingy, the couch was worn out, and Unique could have sworn that she had seen more than twenty roaches since she entered the home.

"You got a boyfriend?" Kiara questioned from out of nowhere.

"Nah."

"Peep this." She whispered so that her mother wouldn't hear. "When my momma leave, we leaving too."

"Where we going?"

"It's Saturday. We going downtown on the Riverfront. All the ballas be down there."

"I can't go. My sista sick."

"She'll be a'ight. You can leave her next door with Miss Mae. She'll take care of her."

"I don't know." Unique shrugged.

"Come on, girl. You only live once," Kay Kay added.

"Patience, do you want to go next door with Miss Mae?"

"Yeah, I like going over her house. She always has food, and her house is clean, plus she be nice to me."

"A'ight then, I guess I'ma go." Unique sprang up from the couch, preparing to leave.

"Uh-uh, you ain't going nowhere with me looking and smelling like that." Kiara scrunched up her nose.

Unique knew she looked a hot mess and smelled an even hotter mess. Her red, green, and orange sleeveless top showcased her dirty bra and brown crumpled deodorant. The orange Guess jeans were two sizes too small, and the Reebok Princesses she wore were so run down that the sole flapped when she walked.

"Well, I don't have anything else to wear, so I guess I can't go." She plopped back down, embarrassed.

"You can borrow something of mine," Kay Kay said, shaking her head at Kiara.

After giving herself and Patience a bath, Unique was fully dressed and ready to go. Dressed in a pink fitted tee, tight jeans, and a pair of clean white K-Swiss, Unique looked hip and more up-to-date. Kay Kay even styled her hair in a weave ponytail to spice up her look.

After dropping Patience off at Miss Mae's, they headed downtown on the bus. The girls weren't even down on the Landing ten minutes before they started getting hollas.

Guys approached Unique left and right, but she turned all of them down because none of them appealed to her. One guy in particular caught her eye, though. He wasn't your best-looking brotha, but his position in the dope game and the money that he brought in every week made him attractive to her. His name was Tone. He sold heroin and embalming fluid, also known on the streets as Water.

Unique saw Tone as her opportunity to make it out of the hood, so she gave him her aunt's number. Tone was a sucka for love, and she fed off that shit. All she had to do was rub his dick and purr in his ear, "I love you," and she got whatever her heart desired.

In a matter of weeks, Unique and Patience moved in with Tone, and she had gotten him to place her mother in one of the best psychiatric hospitals in Missouri.

Now, don't get it twisted. Tone wasn't a pushover. Unique respected his gangsta.

A year into their relationship, she got Tone to rent her a loft in downtown St. Louis, which cost twenty-five hundred dollars a month. Unique also got him to furnish her brand new home with furniture from Bang & Olufsen. After getting her GED, she even got Tone to pay her way through school while she took classes at the University of Missouri–St. Louis. Trips to Paris and Milan with twenty-five thousand dollar shopping sprees were what came next.

Unique thought she had hit the jackpot, but slowly she saw that nothing in life comes cheap. Everything was cool between the two of them, until Tone got possessive. He expected Unique to cater to his every need, while he continued to lie and cheat. After being together for five years, Unique was slowly becoming tired of Tone and their whole situation.

Tired of reminiscing, Unique let the cab driver know that she was ready go.

"Hey, Jeffrey," Unique spoke to the doorman as she got out of the cab.

"Good evening, Unique."

"Has Patience arrived home yet?"

"Yes, ma'am. She arrived about an hour ago. Mr. Robertson is also waiting for you upstairs."

"Thank you." Pressing 10 on the elevator, Unique couldn't wait to get in her bed and go to sleep, but first she had to deal with Tone. She hadn't forgotten about what she had heard earlier from Patience. Getting off on her floor, she pulled out her keys and opened the door to her place.

"What the fuck took you so long?" Tone asked while sitting on the couch, flicking the remote control.

There he was, the nigga she had been playing for the past five years, sitting on her couch with his pants unbuttoned, watching television. Looking at him, Unique wondered why she had stayed with him so long. Yes, Tone was attractive in his own way. He was dark-skinned with smooth waves in his hair and a muscular build, but his ways made him uglier and uglier every day. He constantly lied to her, but Unique, being the chick she was, continued to stay with him. She didn't care if he lied and cheated. He took care of her, and that was all that mattered. Rolling her eyes at him, she stomped her feet and entered her spacious living room, which was decorated with Parisian art.

"Who the fuck are you talkin' to? And button up your pants!"

"Just answer the fuckin' question."

Pausing for a second, Unique tried to pull herself together before she went off. "I stopped by my old hood. Where is my sister?"

"She's upstairs doing her homework. Why you go by there?"

"Because I wanted to see if it still looked the same. Why you all up in my business?"

"How much of my money did you spend while you were in L.A.?" Tone yawned as he buttoned up his pants.

"I didn't spend any of your money," Unique snapped while taking off her shoes.

"You need to quit that shit. When you get locked up, don't come crying to me. I don't understand why you feel the need to steal anyway. It ain't like I don't provide for you."

"You will never be able to give me as much as I can steal," Unique shot, getting up.

"Whatever."

"Yeah, whatever." She paused for a second and continued. "So, I heard you were at Toxic last night acting a fool—popping bottles, buying drinks for everybody, smoking weed, fuckin' with hoes. You did your thing, huh?"

"Don't start."

"Nah, nigga, don't you start! I know you were with Robin last night."

"You don't even know what you're talkin' about."

"Yes, I do. Patience told me," Unique shouted as he followed her up the spiral staircase.

"Man, Patience don't know what she talkin' about."

Ignoring him, Unique poked her head into her sister's room and said, "Hey, baby sis."

"Hi!" Patience jumped. She sat on the edge of her white canopy bed wearing nothing but a towel. Unique figured she'd just gotten out of the shower, so she told her she'd talk to her later. Tone still had to be dealt with.

"Why don't you just tell the truth for once in your life? It's not like this the first time I've found out about you and another bitch," Unique snapped as she walked into her bedroom. Not ashamed of her body, she stood in the middle of her room during broad daylight and took off her clothes.

"Come on, ma, don't start. You know I love you. You're the only one who has my heart." Tone eyed her body hungrily.

Unique's body was the shit. It had more dips and curves than a roller coaster. Her breasts sat up like two plump pillows, while her stomach was as flat as the late R&B singer Aaliyah's. Her hips were perfectly round, only slimming down to define her well-toned calves, but the best part of all was her ass. Unique had the perfect stripper's butt. It wasn't big enough to place a drink on it, but it was fat enough to catch the male species' attention.

"Are you done? 'Cause I ain't tryin' to hear that shit," she said as she turned on the shower.

Tone stood at the bathroom door, watching her. She didn't even close the semi-frosted shower door. She wanted him to see what he had been missing. Tone could feel his dick getting harder by the second as he stood and watched her bend over to lather her legs, only to stand up again and lather her breasts. By the time Unique got under the flow of water and the soap disappeared from her body, his dick was at full attention. She noticed it after she turned off the shower and stepped out.

He handed her a towel, and she wrapped it around herself as she tried to move past him. "Move, boy," Unique said as she bumped into him and made her way to the bed. She got underneath the sheets with nothing on.

"So, you not gon' let me explain?"

"Look, I'm about to go to sleep. Call me later." Unique pulled the covers over her head.

"I ain't through talkin' to you." Tone snatched the covers from her body.

"What are you doing?" she asked, annoyed.

"You gon' listen to what the fuck I got to say."

Being a typical man, Tone thought that sex would solve everything. With both of her thighs in his hands, he slid Unique's body toward the edge of the bed. It had been two days since he had tasted her pussy. Just the sight of her perfect pink clit made his dick hard. Tone had to hit it.

Playing right along with him, Unique massaged her breasts as he placed himself in between her legs. "Ahh!" Unique squealed as Tone feasted on her kitty cat.

One good thing about Tone was that he gave some mean head. No matter how mad she was at him, whenever he went down on her, Unique always forgave him. The way he licked, probed, and sucked her clit all at once satisfied her to the fullest.

Inserting three of his fingers into her pussy, Tone finger-fucked Unique into convulsions. She came so hard that her juices were not only in his mouth but around it as well.

"Where your rubbers at?" he asked out of breath, still holding her thighs in place.

"Why?"

"'Cause we getting ready to fuck."

"Noooo, we're not." Unique smirked, getting up.

"Why not?"

"You think I'm gon' let you hit this after you fucked that bitch Robin? Nigga, please. You got me fucked up."

"Oh, it's like that?"

"What? You ain't know?"

"I'm up. I ain't got time for this shit. I'ma call you later." Tone wiped his mouth and left.

"Please don't!" she yelled after him.

Happy that she busted a nut, Unique turned over onto her side and slid off into a deep sleep. Five minutes later the phone rang.

"Hellooo?" Unique answered the phone, aggravated.

"Damn, ma, what's with the attitude?" Cezar asked.

"It's nothing. What's good wit' you?"

"Handling a little business. You still coming to my man Bigg's coming home party tonight?"

"Yeah. What time does it start?"

"The club opens up at nine o'clock, but we won't be there until eleven."

"A'ight, me and the girls will swing through," Unique assured before hanging up. She grabbed her alarm clock off the nightstand, set the alarm, and pulled the covers over her head until it was time to get up.

Even though it was Bigg's coming home party, you would have thought it was Unique's the way everybody showered her with attention. The girl couldn't help it—she got love everywhere she went. Standing in the middle of the club, she and Zoë grooved to the beat of Lloyd Banks' "On Fire."

Kiara was there too. The two had made up. As soon as she realized what a mistake she was making, Kiara had called and apologized.

With the music pumping, neon lights dancing across the room, balloons and champagne flowing, Unique did her thing. She was backing it up on some dude that she didn't even know. His hands were all on her ass, but she didn't care. All eyes were on her, and she gave the crowd just what they wanted—a show. Without hesitation, Unique took it down to the floor and popped her coochie like she was starring in a Luke video. Easing her way back up, dressed in a lemon yellow, plunging V-neck Versace dress, Unique turned around and busted into the Mono. If Unique could do one thing, it was dance, and she knew it.

Hot and perspiring, she headed to the restroom to freshen up once the DJ switched from "On Fire" to the Ying Yang Twins' "Salt Shaker." Back to the VIP section, with a smile on her face, Unique took her place beside Cezar and the girls. Sipping on a glass of bubbly, she bobbed her head to the sound of the beat, but Unique couldn't have been more miserable. She had a big-dick nigga who gave her any and everything that she wanted, but still she wasn't happy. That was, until Bigg walked through the door.

It was like something straight out of a music video. He came into the club and took over the spot. Every chick in the place had her eyes glued to him, even Unique. Sexy, confident, and cocky were not the words to describe him. Bigg was the pretty type. You know the kind—sexy than a muthafucka. His presence alone demanded your attention. Once you saw Bigg, everything about him would forever be embedded in your mind. Plain and simple, he was that nigga.

"Yo, who is shorty over there sittin' next to your boy?" Bigg's partna NaSheed pointed out.

"I don't know, but mami lookin' kinda right," Bigg replied, massaging his chin as he eyed Unique.

"Yeah, homegirl is the truth."

With both of them in full view of one another, sparks began to go off. He was in Timbs; she was in Manolos. He rocked his clothes like a prince from Harlem; she rocked her gear the fly way—a little Paris runway mixed with a little street chic flava. Bigg was rose-golded out, and Unique was draped in diamonds. They were perfect for one another. Anybody with eyes could see that.

Donned in an all-black Billionaire Boys Club T-shirt and baggy Evisu jeans, the man turned heads. With an all-black STL hat on his head and a pair of black leather Timbs on his feet, Bigg bopped over to the VIP section. For him to have just gotten out of jail, the boy looked damn good. Unique tried her hardest not to stare, but her eyes just wouldn't focus on anything else.

Bigg's outfit complemented his mocha-colored skin, thick eyebrows, brown eyes, connecting beard and mustache, kissable lips, and braids. He stood about six feet two and weighed one hundred and eighty pounds. His body was built like an Adonis. He even had his name tattooed on the side of his neck. The man looked like he'd fuck a nigga up.

"What's really hood?" he yelled as he bopped toward Unique and Cezar.

"Look at this nigga," Cezar said, getting up to give Bigg a hug. "What took you so long to get here?"

"You know a nigga had to cut something first." Bigg grinned while stroking his chin.

"I feel you, but let me introduce you to the team. That big-head muthafucka right there in the throwback is Yayo."

"What up, homey?" Yayo spoke, taking a pull from a freshly lit blunt.

"What up?" Bigg said with a head nod.

"I think Bice and that nigga Stu out on the dance floor tryin' to mack."

"Oh, yeah," Bigg mumbled, transfixed on the caramel honey sitting in front of him.

"Yeah, but fuck them. This the star playa on the team right here." Cezar pointed to Unique. "Unique, this is Bigg. Bigg, this is Unique."

"Nice to meet you." She extended her hand and smiled.

"What's up, ma?" Bigg smiled too, showing off a mouth full of platinum teeth. He had four on the top row of his mouth.

Feeling the heat radiating off of the two, Cezar broke up their little show immediately.

"Ay, Cez, this my man NaSheed. You remember him, don't you?" Bigg continued.

Looking over at Kiara, Unique saw that she was already on NaSheed. Checking him out from head to toe, Unique agreed that NaSheed was a tender.

"Yeah, I remember dude."

"What's up?" NaSheed said, giving Cezar a pound.

"Shit, another day, different dollar."

"Ahem!" Kiara cleared her throat.

"What's the problem, ma? You got something caught in your throat?" NaSheed asked.

"Nah, baby, I'm just tryin' to get your attention."

"Oh, you got my attention a'ight." He took a seat next to her.

"So, what's the deal, homeboy? You ready to get this shit crackin' or what?" Cezar handed Bigg a bottle of Patrón.

"Nigga, you ain't said nothing but a word."

"Excuse me, but I'm getting ready to get another drink. Y'all want anything?" Unique asked both of them. Cezar shook his head.

"Nah, shorty, I'm straight," Bigg replied.

"A'ight, I'll be right back."

"Damn, the game done changed that much since I've been gone?" Bigg asked as he watched Unique's ass bounce as she walked away.

"What you talkin' about, Bigg?"

"You got chicks working for you now?"

"Ay, dog, don't sleep. Li'l momma doing her thing. I trained her up right. Y'all might be working together, so be cool."

"Yeah, a'ight, if you say so."

Bigg tried his damnest to hold a conversation with Cezar but was unable to get his mind off of Unique. To him she was the ultimate chick. Not only was she sexy as hell, but she was on the grind just like he was. There weren't too many females that he could say that about.

"Nigga, is you listening to me?" Cezar asked Bigg, trying to get his attention.

"My bad. What you say?"

Peeping the situation, Cezar wrapped his arm around Bigg's shoulder and said, "Hang it up. You can't pull her."

"What?"

"Nigga, you know what the fuck I'm talkin' about. Unique is priceless. I taught her everything she knows. You my boy and all, but ain't no way in hell she gon' fall for a nigga like you."

"How you gon' try and play me like that?"

"Hey, I'm just stating the facts. We both know that back in the day you was the biggest ho in St. Louis, so whatever game you was planning on kickin' to her, you can hang it up, 'cause Unique ain't fallin' for it."

"I'm glad I know now that you ain't got no faith in yo' boy. I'm straight up feelin' shorty. Mami got a nice swagger about her."

"It's whatever if you gon' holla at her, but don't say I ain't warn you."

"Are you done?" Bigg asked, ready to handle his B.I.

"A'ight, don't say I didn't warn you!" Cezar yelled after him as he went to find Unique.

It didn't take much to find her. She stood out amongst the slew of chicken heads and skeezers.

Unique was standing at the bar when she noticed Bigg approaching her. Seeing him coming near, she blushed on the inside. She had hoped that he would follow her. The chemistry between the two was just too strong for either of them to deny.

"Yo' man gon' get to trippin' you keep on staring at me like that," he whispered in her ear as he wrapped his arms around her waist.

"Boy, please." She laughed, feeling his dick in between her ass cheeks, and the burner that lay on his waist in her back. "And why are your hands on me?"

"Correction, my arms are wrapped around you." He grinned. Releasing his arms from her waist, Bigg stood back, giving her space.

"What you drinkin'?"

"A blue muthafucka. Why?"

"Let me get a blue muthafucka and a Hennessy and Coke," he told the bartender.

Unique tried not to, but she couldn't help but stare at him. The man was amazing.

"See, there you go again. Why you keep staring at me like that?"

"Ain't nobody lookin' at you." She smirked, turning her head.

"Yes, you were. I saw you."

"How was I staring at you?" She turned back and looked him dead in the eyes.

"You lookin' at me like you want a nigga."

Not able to lie, Unique said nothing, knowing he was telling the truth. Being that close to him and catching a glimpse into his brown eyes, she saw a man full of promise and pain. With one look, he made her want to forget about stealing cars and playing men. From that moment on, all she would want was him.

"Oh, so I'm right?" Bigg handed her the drink.

"Thank you. And even if you were right, it doesn't mean anything. You just got home from doing a seven-year bid, and you're trying to fuck anything with a pulse. So, let me tell you something, *Mr. Bigg*. If you haven't noticed already, I'm not like most chicks. A couple lines out yo' mouth and a shiny chain is not gonna do it for me, so try again."

"Are you serious?"

"Damn right I'm serious."

"Do you know how fuckin' ridiculous you sound? You don't even know me," he snapped, getting heated.

"I don't have to know you. All y'all niggas is alike." Unique stood her ground. She didn't know it, but she was fuckin' with the wrong one. She couldn't talk that slick shit with Bigg and get away with it like she did with Tone. He was about to set her ass straight.

"Get the fuck outta here with that bullshit. You know you played yourself, ma, 'cause for a minute there I actually thought I saw something in you, but I guess I was wrong. You just like all of these other hoes in here who only want a nigga for what they got."

"Excuse me?"

"You heard me. Kick rocks, ma. Beat it."

"Nigga, please! Fuck you, wit' yo' broke ass."
Unique rolled her eyes and walked away.

"Who was that you was over there arguing
wit'?" Zoë questioned.

"That was Cezar's punk-ass friend Bigg that
just came home from jail."

"Girl, you trippin. He fine as hell, lookin' like
Young Buck. You better fuck him before I do."

"Trust me, you can have him. He's a lame!"
Unique yelled while looking over her shoulder,
hoping that Bigg could hear her. He could, and
he was staring right at her.

"Yeah, a'ight. Don't be mad when you call me
and I say I can't talk 'cause he got his dick in my
mouth," Zoë joked.

"Girl, shut up. Let's go dance."

Two hours later, the club was letting out and
the party was over. Standing outside in front
of the club, everyone was busy trying to think
of where to go next. Unique hadn't been out
clubbing in months, so kicking it until six in the
morning was the only thing on her mind.

Running, Unique caught up with Cezar before
he got into his truck, to see where he was going.

Unbeknownst to her, one of her diamond earrings had fallen out of her ear.

"Where y'all getting ready to go?"

"We're heading over to the Pink Slip. Why?" Cezar replied.

"I thought we were going to hit up another club."

"Nah, you know my man just coming home. We tryin' to see some ass and titties tonight."

"Eww, whatever. I'ma holla at you later then." Unique scrunched up her face, giving him a hug good-bye.

Disappointed with the change of events, Unique poked her bottom lip out and got into the car with Zoë and Kiara. Fifteen minutes later, they were pulling up to her building.

"A'ight, I'ma holla at y'all later," Unique said, getting out of the car. Both Zoë and Kiara said good-bye.

Riding up the elevator, she reflected back on Bigg and how fine he was. Deep down she was disappointed at how things had turned out. Closing the door a little harder than usual, Unique startled her sister.

"Unique, is that you?" Patience asked as she entered the house.

"Yeah, did anybody call me?"

"Yeah," Patience replied, coming down the steps. Staring at her li'l sister, Unique could only smile. She was the spitting image of their mother. Pretty, with caramel-colored skin, chinky eyes, and a bad shape, Patience had it going on. "How was the party?"

"It was cool." Unique sighed, plopping down on the couch. She hated to admit it, but the girl was beat. "Did the money get here yet?"

"Yeah, it came while you were 'sleep earlier. Tone called you about ten times, too."

"Fuck that nigga. He can keep calling, but enough about him. What's going on with you?"

"Nothing. I've just been having a lot of stuff on my mind lately."

"Well, whatever it is, you know you can talk to me about it, right?"

"Yeah . . . it's just complicated, that's all."

"I'm not going to pressure you, but whenever you're ready to talk, I'm here."

"Okay. Are we going to see Mommy this weekend?"

"Yep."

"I can't wait. I miss her." Patience got up from the couch.

"Me too. Are you going to bed?"

"Yeah. I'm going to church tomorrow with Miss Mae."

"That woman know she love you."

"You're not going to bed?"

"Nah, not yet."

"Well, all right. Love you."

"Love you too."

Looking around the room, Unique examined her spacious loft. The first time she had seen it, she knew she had to have it. She had never seen anything like it. The ceiling and floors were wooden, and the walls were painted a deep orange color, which gave off a sensual vibe. The cream-colored sectional, brown throw pillows, glass table, wooden ottoman, plants, and art set off the entire living room.

In front of the oversized windows, Unique stood and gazed over the city of St. Louis. Every night she thanked God for allowing them to live in a place as beautiful as their home, but she would trade it all in a second if she could have her mother back. Nobody knew how unhappy Unique was, except for Patience. Unique didn't confide in anyone about her true feelings, not even her cousins.

To them she had a perfect life, if you could call stealing cars and playing men for their money a perfect life. Unique had men that provided her and her sister with whatever they wanted without question. Women were dying to be in her position, and she would gladly give it up if she didn't have to support her little sister.

Checking her watch, Unique saw that it was going on three o'clock in the morning, so she decided to head upstairs for bed. Too tired to put on any pajamas, Unique peeled off her clothes and climbed into bed naked.

Over on the east side of St. Louis, Bigg sat with a drink in his hand and a stripper on his lap, but he couldn't get the thought of Unique out of his mind. He couldn't quite put his finger on it, but something about her was very intriguing.

With her in mind, he pulled out the earring that had fallen from her ear back at the club. Bigg couldn't help but grin. Looking at it brought back their entire conversation. Unique's mouth was a little out of control, but he knew that with a little thug love, he could fix that problem.

She was the flyest chick he had ever seen. Even though her looks resembled that of your typical girl next door, there was a roughness about her that intrigued the hell out of him. He wanted to get to know her, see what was in her head.

Tired of the club scene, Bigg decided he was ready to go home, so he tossed the broad on his lap a twenty and told her to get up.

"Where you going?" Cezar questioned.

"I'm getting ready to burn out but, ah, where shorty live at?"

"Who?"

"Unique, nigga, that's who."

"You just won't give up, will you?"

"It ain't even nothing like that. She dropped something back at the club, and I want to give it to her."

"Yeah, right. She stay downtown on Washington in the Merchandise Mart building."

Less than five minutes later, Bigg was on the highway headed back downtown.

Knocked out, dreaming of fucking Bigg, Unique was awakened by the sound of someone beating on her front door. Pissed off because she had been in a good sleep, Unique jumped out of bed, grabbed her robe, and headed for the stairs.

"Who is it?" she asked, sounding a little hoarse.

"Bigg."

Startled, she stood shocked for a second. "How you know where I stay? You some kinda stalker or something?"

"Never that, sweetheart. Cezar told me where you stayed. Your earring fell out while we were standing outside the club, so I figured I'd bring it to you."

Reaching up, Unique felt her ear; her earring was gone. Quickly she unlocked the door and came face to face with Bigg. She couldn't get over how fine he was. Bigg was the kind of nigga that you wanted to go half on a baby with.

"You know you got a smart-ass mouth." He eyed her up and down lustfully.

"Take it or leave it. That's just how I am." She snatched her earring from his hand.

"You're welcome," he said sarcastically while staring at her body.

Bigg had never seen a body like Unique's. She was perfectly proportioned in all the right places. Her robe was short, so he had a perfect view of her thighs and legs. For a minute, he allowed himself to wonder how they would feel wrapped around him.

Just when he thought it couldn't get any better, the top of her robe slightly opened, revealing one of her honey-colored breasts. Her brown, round areola was staring him smack dab in the face and begging him to come suck it. It took everything in Bigg to control himself. His dick was harder than a muthafucka.

"Thank you." Noticing his eyes on her chest, she realized that her robe was open. Embarrassed, she pulled it together again.

"If you're done staring at my breasts, I was asleep," Unique stressed, standing back on one of her legs with her hand on her hip.

"What breasts? I know you ain't talkin' about those little bitty muthafuckas," he joked.

"What you say?"

"Nothing. I'ma check you later, shorty." Bigg laughed some.

"Yeah, whatever!" Unique slammed the door in his face.

Back upstairs in her bedroom, writhing in embarrassment over Bigg seeing her breast, Unique sat on the edge of the bed with her face in her hands. She couldn't get Bigg's eyes out of her mind. His eyes had shown more intensity and desire in just a split second than any other man she had ever known. Unique knew that she had to stay away from him before she ended up doing something she had no business doing.

A couple of weeks had passed since Bigg's party, and things in Unique's life had gotten back to normal. Business was booming, and she and the girls were in and out of town at least twice a month. Sitting on Cezar's couch, Unique flipped through the latest issue of *Us Weekly* magazine while chewing a piece of spearmint gum.

Over the years, she and Cezar had built a very close friendship. Unique proved herself to be a ride or die chick. Cezar respected her gangsta. He respected her so much that he gave her the keys to his house. Only she and his mother had a set. Looking around his crib, Unique had to admit Cezar was doing the damn thing.

His $565,000 home in Chesterfield held a spacious living room, gourmet kitchen, three bathrooms, four bedrooms, a game room, and an outdoor pool. Sitting down on his Mesa leather sectional, Unique ran her hands across the butter-soft material. The Sanibel coffee table that she had picked out years before sat in the middle of the floor. On top of it was an exotic, apple-green vase filled with white calla lilies.

Irritated, she checked her watch and wondered what was taking him so long. Cezar had asked her to meet him at his house at two o'clock for a meeting. Looking at her watch, she saw that it was now going on three o'clock. If Unique had one pet peeve, it was when people were late and didn't bother to call. Hearing footsteps nearing the door, Unique continued to read the magazine, pissed off.

"Took you long enough!" she yelled over her shoulder without looking up.

"My bad. Me and Bigg lost track of time."

Hearing his name caused Unique's heart to drop out of her chest. She didn't know what it was about him, but the nigga had her going. Playing it cool, she continued to act mad.

"Next time call. You know I hate to wait."

Taking a seat across from her, Bigg scoped out Unique's physique while she pretended to ignore him. She looked fly as hell. Her all-black Gucci glasses shielded her eyes, but everything else on her was exposed for all to see. Her reddish blonde hair was flat-ironed bone-straight to the back, and MAC clear lip gloss adorned her lips.

She wore an all-black wife beater, which exposed her full breasts and read *Rich Bitch*, a pair of black 7 For All Mankind booty shorts that showcased her thick butterscotch thighs and legs, and on her feet were a pair of black patent leather Yves Saint Laurent stilettos. Bigg had to admit the chick was bad.

"You can't speak?" he asked.

"Hi," she spoke dryly.

Bigg could only shake his head and laugh. Sitting in his favorite spot on the couch, Cezar leaned forward and began to speak.

"I got a job for you two."

"What is it?" Unique asked, perplexed, taking off her glasses. She never did a job without the girls.

"I'm switching my supplier."

"Why? What's wrong with Jose?"

"Jose be on some bullshit. All of sudden this nigga going up on his prices. Ain't no way in hell I'm gon' pay twenty five Gs a brick when I can get 'em for fifteen from my man Jackson down in Louisiana."

"So, what you need me and Unique to do?"

"I need for y'all to go down there and set everything up. I have the car and hotel already set up for you. You'll be leaving Thursday night, and I expect you back by Sunday afternoon."

"Why can't we be in and out? I ain't trying to be down there the entire weekend with this nigga." Unique scrunched up her face, agitated.

"Yo, ma, what's the deal? You got a problem with me or something?" Bigg asked, heated. He had enough of her and her smart mouth.

"Yeah, I got a problem wit' you. I got my own li'l thing going on. I don't want to be bothered wit' yo' crazy-lookin' ass."

"Check it, ma. I've been making moves since you was in a training bra. You and your li'l gang of car-thieving friends ain't seen half the dough I've seen, so don't get it twisted. You will show me some respect."

Appalled, Unique sat quietly. She couldn't think of anything else to say. The only thing she could come up with to do was suck her teeth, roll her eyes, and say, "Whatever."

"Both of y'all need to calm down." Cezar laughed. "Whatever animosity you two got against each other needs to be put aside. I need your full cooperation." He looked at them both.

"I still don't think this is going to work," Unique mumbled, picking at her fingernail.

"Did I mention that both of y'all will be paid twenty Gs?"

"You should've said that at first." Unique hopped up, grabbing her Bottega Veneta purse, preparing to leave. Placing her shades back on, she gave Bigg one last look and left.

Even though he tried not to notice it, Bigg couldn't keep his eyes off of Unique's big ass.

"I guess everything is set then." Cezar got up too.

Pulling up to the parking lot of the clinic in which her mother lived, Unique looked in the rearview mirror and sighed. It was Family and Friends Friday. Every other week she and Patience would try to attend. Unique dreaded her visits with her mother. Every time she saw her, something bad would happen.

It never failed. After ten minutes of being in the same room with Unique, Syleena would have a fit. She never had one when it was just

Patience. Syleena could sit for hours in complete silence and never utter a word, but when Unique entered the room, all hell would break loose. Unique didn't know what it was that triggered those negative emotions in her mother. Maybe it was her father.

When Unique was younger, Syleena often told Unique that she was the spitting image of him. Whenever Syleena looked at Unique, she remembered the rape. As a child, Unique didn't know how to handle hearing things like that. It made her feel dirty and unwanted.

"Come on. Let's go get this over with," she said as she unlocked her door.

"Don't be like that, Nique. Maybe this time things will be better," Patience reassured.

"Yeah, we'll see," Unique mumbled underneath her breath.

As she walked down the cold, beige-colored corridor to her mother's room, Unique could feel the air in her lungs begin to fade. Seeing her mother had this effect on her, and she didn't like it one bit. Her main purpose in life was to always keep it together and to never let her real feelings show, but when Unique was around her mother, it was like she was instantly zapped back to being a little girl, unable to defend herself from her mother's hurtful words and violent tirades.

"There go my girls," Nurse Sandy spoke.

"Hey, Sandy." Unique smiled halfheartedly. "How you been?"

"Good. How you doing, Miss Honor Roll Student?" Nurse Sandy said, referring to Patience.

"I'm doing good."

"Well, look, your mother's been waiting on you. She's been talking about seeing you all day. Why don't you go see her while I talk to your sister for a bit?"

"Okay," Patience replied as she turned and walked into her mother's room.

"Did she say anything about wanting to see me?" Unique asked, already knowing the answer.

"No . . . not this time, Unique. She'll come around, though."

"Uh-huh, but what is it you need to talk to me about? Tone paid the bill, right?"

"Yes. Tone paid the bill, but we'll talk about him later. Come sit down with me." Nurse Sandy ushered Unique over to a nearby couch.

"It must be something bad. What happened?"

"We did an exam on your mother the other day, and—"

"And what?" Unique asked, becoming impatient.

"The doctors think your mother might have brain cancer."

"What?"

"We didn't want to alarm you until we had all the facts, but for the past two weeks your mother has been having hallucinations. At first we thought it was just her acting out because of her schizophrenia, but then the seizures began. She's had two in the past week. The doctors did a CT scan on her and found a tumor on her occipital lobe."

"I can't believe this." Unique sat with a stunned look on her face.

"Now we're going to do all we can to help her, but with your mother's mental health, it's going to be hard."

"How am I going to tell Patience this?"

"I don't know, but you're going to have to be strong for her, Unique. She's really gonna need you now," Nurse Sandy said, wrapping her arm around Unique's shoulder.

"This is just too much for me to handle right now." Unique let out a loud sigh.

"Just pray, Unique. Everything's gonna be all right."

"Thanks, Sandy."

"You're welcome, sweetie. Now go on in there and see about your momma."

It took everything in Unique not to buckle over and fall as she stood up. She was so hurt by the news of her mother's illness that she didn't know which way was left or right. Standing on the outside of her mother's door, Unique glanced in and watched as Patience and Syleena laughed and talked like two old friends. Unique and Syleena never had conversations like that.

She hated to feel jealousy toward her sister, but Unique often found herself envying Patience. She wondered what it felt like to have their mother look upon her adoringly or to laugh at the things she said. Syleena was always so happy to see Patience. When she saw Unique, the only thing she saw were the eyes of her rapist. Now Syleena was sick, and Unique knew that she may never get to have the healthy relationship with her mother that she prayed for as a child.

"Hey, Momma," Unique spoke as she entered the room.

Each time she visited her mother, Unique was amazed by how beautiful she was and how much Patience took after her. Anyone that looked at her mother could tell that she was a knockout in her day. She had the prettiest caramel, kissed-by-the-sun skin; long, thick hair; and the most alluring brown eyes that anyone had ever seen, but as the years went by and her illness became worse, Syleena's looks seemed to diminish.

"Patty Cake, will you get me a glass of water?" Syleena said, ignoring Unique's presence.

"Sure thing, Momma."

"So, Momma, how you been?" Unique asked once again, trying to spark up a conversation.

"Here you go, Ma." Patience handed Syleena her cup.

"Thanks, Patty Cake. You so good to Momma."

"Momma, I know you hear me!" Unique snapped.

"Is that man with you?" Syleena asked calmly.

"What man, Momma?"

"That damn daddy of yours."

"How many times do I have to tell you that I don't even know who my father is?"

"Come on, Ma, you were doing good. Try to be nice today," Patience pleaded.

"Yeah, Momma, I missed you. I even brought you a present." Unique opened up her purse and pulled out a small jewelry box. Opening it up, she revealed a white gold necklace with a small heart pendant attached. "See, here, it's a locket. It has a picture of me and Patience in it."

"Get that damn thing away from me!" Syleena screamed, slapping the jewelry box away. "Patty Cake, help me! She's trying to hurt me again!"

"No, she's not, Momma. Unique's trying to be nice. Please calm down."

"Don't you see she's the devil? She's just like her father, a Satanist!"

"Momma, no, I'm not. I wish you would quit saying that!" Unique yelled, aggravated and hurt by her mother's words. "I love you. Why can't you see that?"

"You're a liaaaaar! You don't love me. You're out to finish what your father started. I'm not stupid. Patty Cake, help me! She's out to get me! Please?" Syleena begged while holding on to Patience's arm.

"You know what? Fuck this! I ain't got time for this shit. I'm sick of you always treating me like this. I am not my father," Unique snapped. She grabbed the jewelry box off the floor and left the room.

"Unique, don't leave," Patience pleaded, following after her.

"Nah, fuck that. I hate her."

"You don't mean that, Nique. Calm down."

"Yes, I do. I'm tired of this shit. I got other things to deal with besides having to deal with her crazy ass. Now go and finish your visit. I'll be in the car." With that said, Unique headed back to the car and cried for what seemed like hours.

3

I Wanna Get 2 Know Ya

It was two o'clock Thursday morning. Unique
sat patiently in her living room, awaiting Bigg's
arrival. He was late. Tapping her foot, she sat
mad as hell. They were supposed to be on the
road by now. Unique tried calling his cell phone,
but each time his voice mail would pick up. This
was the very reason she didn't work outside her
circle. At least with the girls she had complete
and utter control.

The past week for Unique could be described
as hell, to say the least. After the disastrous
meeting at the clinic with her mother, more bad
news came in. The doctors called and confirmed
that Syleena indeed had brain cancer. The only
thing Unique could do was break down and cry
upon hearing the news.

She regretted everything she'd said that day.
She was just so frustrated by the news of her

mother possibly having cancer and by her mother's behavior that it all just became too much for her; but Unique, being the chick she was, managed to somehow bring it all back together. She and Bigg had a job to do, and she couldn't let her mother's illness get in the way and fuck up her head.

Speaking of Bigg, after doing some background digging, Unique learned that before he got locked up, he was doing it real big. He grew up on the south side of St. Louis with Cezar. They both attended the same high school—Roosevelt. Bigg was a good guy. He played basketball his entire time in school, but his dreams of making it to the NBA were dashed when he busted his knee during a game. Bigg was crushed. Playing ball was supposed to be his ticket out of the hood.

Since his dreams of playing ball were no longer in reach, he turned to the streets. Cezar was already in the game, so it was only natural that Bigg linked up with him. Cezar introduced Bigg to the drug game. They both sold girl and boy, but as time passed, Bigg gained more territory than Cezar. Cezar wasn't the jealous type, but no matter how hard he tried, he could never bring in a fourth of Bigg's cheese.

Bigg had everything that Cezar wanted: real estate all over St. Louis, two barber shops, liquor stores, a beauty salon, five luxury cars, celebrity friends, and around that time, he had even ventured into the music industry. Business was booming for Bigg. He was living the high life of a young, rich, black bachelor—that was, until he was pulled over with ten kilos of cocaine in the trunk of his car. Bigg was seventeen years old and sentenced to ten years in prison, but he only ended up serving seven. With Bigg gone, Cezar took over and began running the streets of St. Louis.

Now fresh out of prison, Bigg was ready to reclaim his spot. He got out of bed, sat on the edge, and looked out into the night sky. The room was pitch black except for the slight glimmer of light shining from the moon up above. It had been seven years since he'd seen the stars. Running his hands down his face, Bigg thanked God once more for bringing him home. This time he was going to do things right. No more jail for him. He would die before he went back.

Since he had been out, Bigg had been making moves left and right. His one and only desire was to regain his crown on the streets. Bigg couldn't stand playing second fiddle to Cezar or any other man. He was grateful that Cezar put him on, but Bigg was used to being his own boss.

As he slipped on his pants and zipped them up, he checked his watch and noticed that he was over an hour late picking up Unique. Bigg knew that he was going to catch hell once he caught up with Unique.

"Baby, where you going?" a young redbone by the name of Brittany purred, half asleep. Poor thing. Bigg had worn the child out. She could barely move after he was done putting it on her.

"A nigga gotta make moves, ma. I'ma holla at you when I get back," he said, pulling his T-shirt on over his head.

"You can't stay a little while longer?" she whined, exposing her honey-colored double-D breasts.

"I wish I could, but I'm late. I gotta be somewhere."

"Okay." Brittany continued to pout.

"I promise when I get back it's me and you." Bigg kissed her forehead.

"Call me!" she shouted after him.

An hour later, just as Unique was about to pick up the phone and call Bigg again, she heard a faint knock on the door. Pissed, she snatched the door open. She shook her head and rolled her eyes. Just the sight of him made her sick.

"Yo, my bad. I got caught up," he tried to explain.

"Yeah, whatever. Let's just go and get this shit over with," Unique said as she pushed past him.

His nasty ass was probably out fuckin' some ho, she thought.

"You're forgetting your bags."

"You can't get 'em for me?"

"Say please."

"Nigga, you got me fucked up. I'll get my own damn bags," she huffed, walking back into her loft. Unique grabbed her heavy luggage, which was filled to the brim with designer clothes, shoes, and accessories, and lugged it onto the elevator with her.

"You a'ight?"

"I'm fine." Unique rolled her eyes as she tried to steady her breathing.

I need to get to the gym, she thought.

"You sure? Those bags look a little heavy." He grinned.

"I said I'm fine."

Unique couldn't wait to be away from him. Bigg was a self-absorbed, arrogant asshole. Standing side by side, she tried not to notice how good he looked. It was a little chilly out, so he sported a gray Enyce jacket, white T-shirt, jeans, and on his feet were a pair of white-and-gray BAPE tennis shoes.

This is gonna be one long weekend, she thought.

Once they reached the main floor, Unique hoped and prayed that Jeffrey was working the night shift. Stepping off the elevator, she spotted him by the door.

"Jeffrey, can you load these bags in the trunk for me?"

"Sure, ma'am."

Once everything was settled, Unique got into the rented white Denali truck. She had no intentions of talking to Bigg, so she placed her seat belt on, slid off her pink Juicy flip-flops, folded her arms, closed her eyes, and drifted off to sleep.

Hating her attitude but loving the way she looked, Bigg smiled, put the key in the ignition, and began their road trip to Louisiana.

Four and half hours into their trip, Bigg turned the volume up on the radio, pulled out a blunt, and sparked it up.

Eightball and MJG's "Don't Flex" was on. He had no choice but to turn it up; it was his jam. Unique was still asleep. Looking over at her, Bigg couldn't help but laugh. Her head was turned to the left, facing him. The girl was snoring, and on top of that, her mouth was hanging wide open. Bigg even spotted a little trickle of drool sliding down the corner of her lower lip.

"Don't flex, baby. . . . I wanna see you touch your toes in that dress, baby. . . . Bounce it up and down like we having sex, baby. . . . ," he sang in between taking pulls off the blunt.

Stretching her arms and legs out, Unique yawned. The smell of Purple Haze in the air and Eightball and MJG on the radio had her fully awake. Feeling that her face was wet, she quickly wiped the side of her mouth.

God, I hope he didn't see that, she thought.

"Where are we?"

"We're in Memphis," he said, passing her the blunt.

"Thanks," she replied, inhaling the smoke into her lungs.

"Yo, you was over there knocked the fuck out, snoring and shit."

"I was not. I do not snore."

"Somebody lied to you, 'cause you was over there snoring like a muthafucka."

"Fuck you." She grinned as her stomach began to growl. "Are you hungry? 'Cause I am."

"Yeah, we can stop."

Denny's was only two miles up the road, so they decided to stop there. She put her flip-flops back on, grabbed her purse, and hopped out of the truck. Bigg was already at the door, holding it open for her.

"Thank you."

"You're welcome," he replied, admiring her ass.

"Hi. Can we have a table for two?" Bigg asked the waitress once inside.

"Sure. Smoking or non-smoking?"

"Non-smoking, please."

"Follow me."

As they walked over to their table, Bigg continued to eye Unique's thick thighs and plump ass as she walked. The jeans she had on were so tight that he swore he caught a glimpse of her pussy print.

After guiding them over to a booth by the window, the waitress, Tracy, gave them both a menu and a glass of water. After ordering, they sat in silence for a minute.

"So, Bigg, what's your real name?" Unique asked, breaking the ice.

"How you know my real name ain't Bigg?"

"I know your momma did not name you Bigg." She laughed.

"It's Kaylin, sweetheart."

Hearing Bigg call her sweetheart caused Unique to blush. She couldn't believe that she had graduated to sweetheart level so fast.

"Kay . . . lin. I like that."

"So, what's up wit' you and Cezar?" he asked out of nowhere.

"Nothing. Why you ask that?"

"I mean, you got keys to the nigga crib and shit. I figured y'all was more than just friends."

"Well, you figured wrong. Cezar and I are *just friends*," Unique stressed, hoping she was making herself clear.

"Okay, so what's up with the attitude then, Miss Unique?"

"What you mean by that?"

"You're so cold and defensive all the time. What nigga hurt you?"

"Ain't no man hurt me. Life hurt me."

"What happened in your life that was so fucked up?"

"Basically, I've been an adult since as far back as I can remember. My mother's been in and out of my life since I was little."

"What, she a blockhead?"

"Nah, my momma ain't on crack. She's schizophrenic. She's in a mental institution out in Jefferson City. I've been raising my li'l sister for the past five years by myself. It's hard, but I love my li'l sister. She's really the only family I have besides my cousins, Kiara, Kay Kay, and Zoë. We try to go visit her at least twice a month."

Out of nowhere, Unique's eyes began to well up with tears as she spoke. She hadn't talked about her mother in years, and all the frustration seemed to start spilling out of her all at once. Looking out the restaurant window, she folded her arms across her chest and willed herself not to cry.

"It's hard, you know . . . because . . . me and my moms don't really get along," she continued.

"And why is that?"

"Because every time she looks at me she sees the man who raped her." Unique turned and looked Bigg square in the eyes. He didn't know what to say. All he could do was sit and looked stunned.

"Yeah, that's right, I'm a product of rape. I don't know who my ol' dude is and don't wanna know. My mother hates me, and I'll use anybody or anything to get what I want, so now you see there ain't shit a man can do to me that life hasn't already done." Unique's lower lip began to tremble.

"It's cool, ma. You can cry. Let that shit out." Bigg reached his hand underneath the table and placed it on her thigh.

"I'm cool." Unique wiped her eyes and slid her leg away. She couldn't believe that she had allowed herself to have a weak moment in front of Bigg. Unique thrived off of keeping everything together and bottled in.

"Well, if you ever need to talk, I'm here."

"I won't," she sniffed.

"Here you go," the waitress said, placing their meals in front of them and interrupting their conversation.

"Thank you. Can I have some ketchup with this?" Bigg asked, ready to tear into his food.

"Sure." The waitress handed him a bottle. "Anything else?"

"No, that's all."

"Ma'am, do you need anything?"

"No, I'm fine," Unique answered without looking up. She didn't want the waitress to know she had been crying.

Taking a bite of his omelet, Bigg wondered if he should continue to pick Unique's brain. He didn't want to dredge up any more horrible memories from her past, so he decided to switch the subject to relationships.

"So, tell me, Unique. You got a man?"

"Yeah, why?" She looked him square in the eyes.

"'Cause I wanted to know."

"We've been together for five years." Taking a bite of her T-bone steak, Unique checked for his reaction.

"Five years?" Bigg was surprised. "Damn, that's a long time. You must love that nigga."

"Actually, I don't." Unique laughed a little bit.

"What? How you gon' be wit' a man for five years and not love him?" Bigg grabbed the salt and shook some onto his omelet.

"Easy." She shrugged her shoulders. "And you shouldn't put salt on your food. You're going to have high blood pressure by the time you're thirty."

"It's cool." He waved her off. "But what you mean, easy? You gotta have some kind of feelings for the dude."

"I mean, he's cool. He gives me whatever I want, and that's all I need from him."

"So, you are one of those chicks who only want a nigga for his ends."

"Look." Unique placed her fork down. "I don't believe in fairy tales and happily-ever-afters. Love will never be in the equation for me."

"And why is that?" Bigg listened closely, dying to hear her answer.

"Think about it. What is love? Love is nothing but an imaginary feeling that people trick themselves into believing."

"You really believe that?"

"You damn right I do. Fuck love."

"Wow. That's harsh."

"That's life. Like I said, fuck love, 'cause love ain't never gave a damn about me."

Not able to argue with that, Bigg finished the rest of his meal in silence. Once they finished eating, he paid the check. Unique was already at the car.

The rest of the trip was cool. After the incident at Denny's, Unique kind of withdrew and put her guard up once again. Bigg could understand the way she felt, so he didn't pry.

Finally, after a ten-hour drive, they reached Louisiana. Unique couldn't wait to see what the Dirty Dirty had to offer. Cezar had booked them separate suites at the historic French Market Inn. The place was absolutely breathtaking. Unique couldn't have been happier. After they checked the car in with the valet service, she and Bigg headed in.

"Hi, my name is Edward Whitaker. I'm here to check in," Bigg lied, using one of his aliases.

"Okay, let me look that up, sir," the desk clerk chimed. "I'm sorry, sir. Your check-in time was for three o'clock. As you can see it's five thirty. One of your rooms has already been taken, but the other room is still available."

"So, what you're saying is that I'm going to have to sleep in the same room with him?" Unique asked, appalled.

"Yes, ma'am, that's the way it looks."

"Oh, hell naw! I can't believe this shit."

"Don't mind her. We'll take it."

This turn of events had thrown Unique for a loop. She didn't know how she was going to survive three days with Bigg, let alone share a bed.

Standing in the elevator on their ride up, she turned to him and said, "While we're in this room together, there will be no funny business. We will not be having sex, so don't even try it."

"Who said anything about having sex?"

"I know how y'all niggas think."

"There you go with that shit again. Evidently me fuckin' you is on your mind. Don't beat around the bush, ma. All you gotta do is ask." Walking up on her, he continued, "You want me to fuck you, Unique?" Her back was up against the elevator wall, pinned by his body, as they exchanged breaths.

"Boy, please. You better get away from me." Unique gazed into his eyes, barely able to breathe.

"That's what I thought." He grinned, backing up. "Trust me, fuckin' you ain't even on my mind. Besides, you wouldn't know what to do with this dick anyway. I'm too much of a man for you to handle. Continue to fuck with these li'l locs, ma, 'cause a nigga like me would tear your shit up and have you begging for more."

"Negro, please. You and that jailhouse dick of yours can kiss my ass," Unique spat as they got off the elevator and walked toward their room.

"You know what? You and that mouth of yours gon' get you fucked up."

"Just open the door."

"That's real talk. I'm gon' end up fuckin' you up before the weekend is over." He inserted the key into the door.

"Whatever." Unique rolled her eyes as she entered their lavish suite.

The room was quite elegant. The style was very dark and sensual. One king-size bed sat in the middle of the floor, while a desk and armoire adorned the wall. Walking farther into the suite, they saw a couch, mini bar, full bath, and Jacuzzi. Plopping down onto the bed, Unique kicked off her shoes and turned on the television. She was so into the Style Channel that she didn't even notice Bigg undressing. Then out of nowhere she caught a glimpse of chocolate flesh.

Quickly turning her head toward him, Unique saw that Bigg had stripped down to his boxers. Holding her breath, she tried not to let the words escape that filled her mind: *Prison did a body good*. Even though Bigg was tall, his body was ripped with muscles. His arms and legs were full, and his abs held a perfect six-pack.

She ran her eyes over his upper torso and noticed several different tattoos. Across his stomach he had the name *Dontay* written in an arch. His left arm had *Bigg Entertainment* written with money and smoke formed around it. On his right forearm was a scripture, and on his hands he had *Bigg* tattooed on one, and the other, *Upps.* As he turned around, she also noticed that he had a huge gash going across his left shoulder blade. It looked like someone had beaten him with a belt or cane. What really caught her eye was a tattoo of a man blowing his brains out.

Ignoring Unique's blatant stares, Bigg continued to undress. He stepped out of his boxers and walked past her like she wasn't even in the room. Unique eyed him hungrily and bit into her lower lip. There was no denying it—she wanted Bigg in the worst way. His thick, ten and a half–inch dick called her name as he bopped toward the bathroom door.

"What are you doing?" she finally asked with a dry mouth.

"What does it look like I'm doing? I'm about to take a shower."

"You couldn't have taken off your clothes in the bathroom?"

"No, why? Is my dick bothering you or something?" He grinned devilishly.

"Boy, please." Unique waved him off, rolling her eyes.

"Admit it, Unique. You want me."

"Bigg, get over yourself. The only person who wants you is a nigga named Stud on cell block eight."

"I see you got jokes," he said, stepping closer. Standing directly in front of her, Bigg rubbed his manhood. Unique looked into his eyes and tried her best not to notice his erection, but it was very hard not to, being that his dick was damn near smacking her in the face.

"Touch it. I know you want to," he whispered.

Unable to resist a big dick, she softly slid her hand from the tip to the shaft. Unique had never seen a dick so big in her life. Bigg was truly living up to his name. Not only did he have length and width, but the muthafucka was heavy as well. The man had a dick the size of an anaconda.

Gazing into each other's eyes, they continued to slide their hands up and down his mammoth penis.

"I knew you wanted a nigga." He laughed, taking his dick from her hand.

Feeling stupid, Unique snapped back to reality and said, "Whatever, nigga. I was trying not to hurt your feelings."

"Quit frontin'. You know you want to drop them drawers."

"Boy, please. You better get yo' ass away from me."

"You can join me in the shower if you want," he suggested, standing in the doorway of the bathroom, giving Unique a perfect view of his muscular ass.

"I'll pass," Unique said, focusing her attention back to the TV.

"Yeah, a'ight. Whatever, ma. Keep lying to yourself."

"Bigg, shut the fuck up and concentrate on not dropping the soap."

♥ ♥

31901059332058